REVEAL ME

THE ATLAS SERIES (BOOK 3)

SAPPHARIA MAYER

EIDYLLIO

Ebook ISBN: 978-1-64893-006-5

Audiobook ISBN: 978-1-64893-008-9

Print ISBN: 978-1-64893-007-2

REVEAL ME

AUTHOR'S NOTE

Dear reader,

I am so glad you picked up my book, and I hope you enjoy the story it weaves. Please remember, theses books are works of fiction. The timelines are compressed, the interactions are dramatic and characters often jump into things for want of adventure.

You, dearest reader, live in a reality where the world is often stranger than fiction and a good dominant or submissive is hard to find. When you do find one, it is quickly evident they are imperfect humans who can't read minds, are less observant than one might prefer, and the interaction with them takes time. Like all things in life, communication is the key to any good interaction. The more authentically open you can be with a partner the more fulfilling the relationship.

Remember you are in charge of your life. Use your safe word, let others know where you are, know what aftercare looks like for you, use protection and have fun. The goal is to live in a beautiful safe, sane and consensual relationship with all parties pulling their weight. It is my hope you all find your special someone, just like the characters in my books. *~Sappharia*

WARNINGS & DISCLAIMERS

CHAPTER ONE

"THROUGHOUT HUMAN HISTORY, there have been exchanges of power. These exchanges are conceptual and physical, both consensual and non-consensual, but those aren't the terms we use for them on a macro scale. The more recognizable terms are family, clan, community or repression, oppression, oligarchy, dictatorships. Each of these represents an exchange of power. Usually that exchange, in a societal concept, is used for safety, security, or to ensure certain needs are met in our own personal hierarchy. Over time they are encoded into the general societal contract and we forget the nature of the power exchange, translating it to the idea of tradition.

"When we take this exact same concept down to the micro, individual and specific community level, we can see the same situations forming. Two, or more, entities in which basic power is inferred, choosing to exchange it by personal agreement." Professor Dominick Dawes pontificates from the stage in the mid-size lecture hall, which is currently full for his Sexuality Studies graduate seminar.

I find a seat in the crowded room, on the back row, when a male student stands up and motions me over.

The hall smells of a combination of coffee, perfume, and a crowd of bodies. The auditorium style hall's seats curve stadium style, rising from the small stage in the center.

A student's hand shoots up to answer Dominick's question.

"Yes, Angela?" Dominick acknowledges the girl.

"Professor, why would anyone give up power?"

"Good question, Angela. Would you like the answer at a macro or a micro level?"

She sits there for a moment thinking. "A micro one."

"Why are you paying money to be in this class?"

"Because I need a degree and they told me I had to take this one or something like it."

"And why do you need a degree, Angela?"

"To get a better job and make more money."

"And why do you need money?"

"To survive. To pay for food, shelter, clothes."

"And the designer handbags your parents won't buy you if you don't go to class?" He nods to the Gucci bag on the floor.

Her head nods lightly.

"So you have entered into a power exchange agreement with your parents and negotiated the continued supply of the lifestyle to which you've become accustomed for as long as you go to school, maintain the appropriate grade, and ultimately get a degree. Correct?"

"Well, when you put it like that," she huffs.

"And who has the power in this exchange, Angela?"

"My parents do. If they cut me off, I'll be lost."

A smile crosses Dominick's face and he looks out across the room.

"Now we understand how the basic concept of a power exchange is applied in the reality of our worlds. There is no exception in the most primal idea of sex. Often people find it very gratifying to overtly exchange power in a sexual relationship. It is the most personal form of trust and intimacy you can share with other human beings.

"To actually exchange power conceptually, both parties must

come to the table with their own power. So what exactly does that mean?"

The room falls silent as Dominick's eyes search each person. His eyes land on me, his face clouding with a mixture of concern and irritation.

"You, in the very back with the hat. Alexandra, I believe it is." He stares at me for a long minute, as if his eyes are deceiving him. The silence causes the entire class to turn toward me to see what has captivated the attention of their professor.

"Sir, it means that all parties involved must actually know and understand themselves and the nature of the power exchange. In layman's terms, the dominant is driving the car while the submissive navigates. If they do not work in tandem and harmony, then at best, they will get nowhere fast and at worst they will irreparably damage the physical body or relationship. It's not about the abuse of power, which is non-consensual at its very base, but rather about the illusion of control, a place where one readily gives and one readily receives an action. The exchange, as in all exchanges, is in the allowing and participation by both parties."

"Long winded as always, but a very accurate analogy." Dominick nods but his face grows sterner.

The class continues to stare openly at me. The fascinator veil falls dark and low, creating a shadow over half my face. My tailored suit fits my body perfectly, presenting an out of place impeccable image.

The interruption is a curiosity and the obvious personal knowledge between Dominick and me piques the interest of the entire class.

"How does this power exchange change our understanding within the concept of sexuality studies?" He works to bring the class back forward, but I know what is coming next. Dominick could never resist walking the line, playing with his young class' curiosity in sexual studies.

"It depends on the individuals involved," I comment aloud. "It could be that it is a fight for the right to participate in a desired activity. In other places, it could be the interruption of gender roles to provide more fluidity outside of the gender normative world. Then again, we could talk about feminist concepts of equality and gender rights, in what some would identify as a lack of power exchange. Or what about the reverse of 'traditional' power, the most common face of which is the Dominatrix and the submissive male or female," I say, inwardly cringing at the term that aroused stereotypes of women in lingerie and leather, impossibly high heels and wielding a whip, which ultimately has little to do with actually being a professional of the craft.

Frustration crosses Dominick's face. I'm not the same controllable student I was when he took on my mentorship, outside the classroom, while I attended Boston University. It is also quite evident that something is wrong. He hasn't seen me dressed this way since I worked for him on the side, and even then I wouldn't dare go out in public.

"I think that's enough for today. Due next class, find a power exchange and defend it or refute it. Typed. Double spaced. APA styling," he says over the rustle of papers.

I sit quietly, watching the students leave the lecture hall. It hasn't been all that long ago that I'd graced these same hallowed halls daily, in pursuit of a greater life. The turns and directions since were amazing and harrowing at times. Even I have to admit I'm not the same girl that left here. Yet I still feel there's something missing.

The click of the phone's camera is barely audible when I look up, causing everything in me to freeze. This is the exact reason I'd worn this outfit. Just in case the constant click of cameras or video, which everyone seems to want to post for some inane reason, does show up, it won't alert anyone of my location.

Everyone seems to have a camera these days. I hope with half my face in shadow the picture will not reveal who I am when it gets posted. There is no debate on "if" because no matter what, it will always be posted. Unfortunately, I'd not been able to prevent

Dominick from calling my name. At least he'd called the one to match the outfit.

Sitting in his class is a dumb risk. I needed something to give me comfort, and listening to Dominick's lecture always gave me solace. It was something about his baritone voice that made me feel secure.

Dominick was my first dominant and trained me in the mental, physical, and emotional techniques of the trade. He was the father figure who gave me the ability to truly understand the underlying movements of the world, making all of my successes possible. In some ways, it also made my fall inevitable.

For the last several weeks I was off the grid completely. No contact with my staff, my friends, or Reece. It's the only way I could ensure their safety on the heels of being stalked by a client and falling in love with a Dominant, causing an internal war of epic portions.

Nothing in my life felt like my own, but I knew if Kade and Samantha hadn't yet tracked me down, then there was no way for Edmund to do it.

———

I watch the hall clear. Students lingering in clusters, periodically looking my way and then conversing in low whispers. On the lecture stage, Dominick fields questions from several students, mostly female, who are all vying for his attention. Periodically his eyes lift, looking to make sure I am still waiting. The look in his eyes glues me to my seat. I remember the look. The one he always gave me when I crossed a line or broke a rule. Taking a deep breath, I wonder for the hundredth time if this is the most intelligent decision I've made today.

When the room is cleared, except for a couple of small clusters of students loitering in the back corners of the hall, Dominick motions me to the stage. We stare at each other for a long moment. His eyebrow quirks in a question, and I know I've pushed my luck a bit too far.

Deliberately I stand, smoothing invisible wrinkles in my suit to fortify my resolve. Everything in me is running on empty. Dominick is the one place where I hope I can hide quietly and recharge.

Straightening up to my full height, I step purposefully and gracefully down each row. I look up to the stage when I reach the bottom. Dominick's eyes bore a hole right through me like my sins are open for his full examination. In every possible way, I've been analyzed and evaluated.

"Come," he commands, motioning to the stage with his hand.

My head drops slightly in practiced deference, and I make my way up the short staircase.

He openly looks me up and down, as if he's calculating his next move, taking in all the information currently provided to him.

"Something's wrong," he states.

"Can't I just come visit? I was in the neighborhood..."

"Stop. You can speak again when you can be honest with me," he says, turning on his heel.

I follow. I know what is expected.

We walk in silence across the stage, stepping out of the door from the lecture hall and down the long corridor toward his office.

He unlocks the door and steps inside. The walls of his office are neatly arranged, with boxes marking their contents above the dark mahogany desk set against the wall of large windows. Shelves line two of the walls, full of books from floor to ceiling. I note the marks going down one leg of the desk. They were placed there for each strike I received when I didn't follow directions, broke a rule or generally needed an attitude adjustment. The line of marks runs from the top of the front of the leg to its bottom. My small initials are barely visible under the lip of the desktop.

"Andrea, cancel my office hours. Something's come up unexpectedly and needs my immediate attention," he says into the phone. "I'll need you to cover the lecture on Thursday."

He listens intently to the reply, turning his stern gaze in my direction. It is the same look he gave me right before I made one of the marks going down his desk leg.

"Thank you, Andrea," he says cordially, placing the receiver down.

Cautiously he turns to me, like I'll spook and run away if he moves too fast.

"Does Kade know you're here?"

"No."

His eyebrow raises.

"No, Sir," I amend.

"Does Samantha know you're here?"

"No, Sir."

"Does anyone know you're here?"

I shake my head, letting it fall forward.

"No, Sir."

Dominick runs a hand through his unruly salt and pepper hair in frustration. There is no doubt he is confused at my sudden presence and angry because he doesn't know why. He hates being out of control or outside the circle of knowledge, and in one fell swoop I've created both.

"Did you pilot yourself?" He continues with the interrogation.

"No, Sir."

"Did you take a leave of absence from the PR firm and the club?"

I shake my head, remembering how I'd set my phone on my desk and simply walked away. Guilt washes over me, but it was the only way I knew how to keep everyone safe. I'd already caused Reece's sister's campaign irreparable damage by keeping my secrets. At least this way Edmund couldn't stalk me here, and there'd be no reason for him to attack anyone else I loved.

"I simply walked away without explanation," I admit, blowing out a breath I didn't realize I was holding.

Dominick nods. "I see."

He grabs a couple of stacks of papers and places them in the leather messenger bag I'd given him when I decided to leave for Washington DC. The sight of it leaves me sentimentally torn.

"Come on, girl. Let's get you home. It looks like we've got quite a bit to talk about," he says, walking out of his office. I follow without the need for a command.

WE ARE QUIET ON THE DRIVE FROM BOSTON UNIVERSITY TO Waltham. Each of us is lost in our own thoughts. Periodically he looks over at me, as if he's trying to figure out an enigmatic puzzle. When he parks outside his apartment, it's six in the evening. Lights blaze in the windows, and I feel like I've suddenly interrupted something. He switches off the engine, sitting quietly for a long moment before turning to me.

"Why are you here, Atlas?"

I stare down at my hands, just like I did when I was in school. My fingers knot together, and the emotions I've held down suddenly feel like they will volcanically erupt if I'm not careful.

"I don't know. Right now I just feel scared and lost. After quite a long wander alone in the wilderness, the only place I wanted to go was home," I admit quietly.

Dominick reaches over, taking one of my hands, giving it a gentle squeeze.

"This isn't home, Atlas. Home is in DC, where your entire world can surround you and give you whatever you need. There's something big you're not telling me, girl, but then again, you're not telling anyone. Whatever it is, we'll figure it out together."

I smile softly. Everything in me wants to believe him. Unfortunately, I am long past the moments where I think he's superhuman. Today, the world actually sits completely on my shoulders.

"Before we go inside, I want to remind you the rules didn't change in your absence. Here, you are not my equal. You may stay under my roof, but you know the price," he states simply. "Do you agree to step back into that place?"

"Yes, Sir."

"Do you remember the signals and commands?"

"I believe so," I reply honestly.

"Then my home is open to you. Do you wish to proceed?"

"Yes, Sir. Thank you," I say simply and watch him get out of the car and walk around to my door.

CHAPTER TWO

WHEN THE DOOR OPENS, I step out. My eyes look up at the large brownstone. This place is both familiar and nightmarish. Need drove me here, but I lack the internal understanding of why.

Ahead of me, Dominick strides to the front door. There is no need for further conversation. I know I am to follow, and he knows I will. The surroundings penetrate my senses and I stand still for too long. At the top of the stairs, he looks down at me and raises an eyebrow. It is all I need to get moving.

The heels of my shoes tap against the stairs as I rise toward the front door. He holds it open, I enter, and he steps in behind me. With unpracticed movements, I slip my shoes off beside the doorframe. Once the door closes behind me, I fall to my knees. Head up, eyes slightly cast down. Just enough to show deference and not too much that I would miss a silent command.

"You dress as a Dominant. A place you relinquished when you entered my household on your knees. A house uniform sits on the bench beside you."

The words are a statement of fact. In this place, I bow to the Master of the house. That is the way here. In many ways, he is still

Master. Maybe a part of me still seeks it or maybe I've come to bury the skeletons. The thoughts run rampant through my head.

"Do you think yourself above such a station?" His sharp tone cuts through my thoughts.

"Nnn...oo, Sir." My normal confidence folds.

"Then move."

With a lack of grace I stand. My fingers fumble over buttons, pins, zippers, and snaps. It is humiliating not to perform the most mundane of tasks without elegance. Just weeks ago, I glided through the club to looks of awe. The power no one questioned. Now all I can think of is my fall to disgrace and the fear which put me in this place.

I pull up the gray pencil skirt and pull the gray polo shirt over my head. The uniform is utilitarian. Meant to strip a person down to the bare essentials and build them up again. In this moment I am nothing. In this place no one can depend on me because I am the lowest of a household. Temporarily, the weight of my world slips from my shoulders.

"Much better. Ana will show you to your room. You will not speak. There is tea and food in your room. At eight o'clock, report to my study for confession."

He turns on his heel and disappears down the hall.

A young woman of twenty-two or so appears before me. Her uniform is similar to mine, but she's earned her colors. It signifies how she's worked her way through a significant amount of self-awareness and understanding under Dominick's tutelage.

Without a word, I follow her up the staircase to the smallest room in the house. It is referred to as the closet, and as its name implies, it was once a walk-in. Now, it houses a twin-size horizontal Murphy bed, which currently looks like a couch. To the left is a meditation mat and to the right, a kneeling desk in the corner. On the far wall is a window and the only light source for the room. When it is dark outside, one must learn their way in the darkness and take advantage of the knowledge gained in the light. The symbolism is subtle but not lost. I've spent many a night of punishment or penance in this room. I can only imagine my fate after the confession.

"There is tea on the desk. I've placed cucumber sandwiches and a small salad on the tray. When I leave, this room will be dark. I am sorry I can't leave you any light, but Master was specific in his instructions. He said you'd know exactly what to do."

I turn and face her, forcing a smile. My head nods.

Using the fading light from the window and the ambient light from the open doorway, I move to the desk. My legs fold under me in a kneel just as the hallway light fades. The evening light from the window casts dark shadows around the room.

I pour a cup of tea and inhale the scent of Creamed Earl Grey, one of my favorites. Knowing he remembered lightens my mood slightly. I grab a sandwich and turn to sit on the floor. Legs not used to kneeling stretch in pain. My stomach growls as I bite into the bread. This is a simple meal of comfort for me. Dominick always rolled his eyes when he asked what a simple comforting meal looked like. He may never have understood, but it was obvious he'd paid attention.

By the shadows on the wall, I estimate it is close to seven o'clock. I know he will send word before my given time in the office. Sated by the food, I let my eyes drift closed.

———

LIGHT HITS MY EYES. I BLINK THEM OPEN AGAINST THE ASSAULT. The surrounding room is pitch dark except for the stream of light spotlighting me.

"It's time," Ana states.

Dread runs through my body. Carefully I stretch and stand to follow her. I always hated confession. They were a way to verbalize all the racing thoughts, confess mistakes, and make tangible the release of failure through physical means rather than holding them inside.

Dominick is a master of the confession. One who can walk the line of finding the truth, even when it isn't clear. This time, however, I know exactly what I'm hiding.

Ana turns, walks down the hall, and heads down the stairs. Without a word I follow. When we approach the French doors to Dominick's office, she makes the silent command to kneel. For a long second, I look at her incredulously, but she doesn't move.

Finally, I nod and kneel at the door entrance. Ana knocks on the door above me.

"Come," Dominick says behind the door, and it opens in front of me. She steps inside and waits in silence.

"Thank you, Ana. You may retire for the evening with free time."

"Thank you, Master." She nods her head in deference, turns precisely on her heel, and walks from the room.

In front of me, Dominick gives the silent command to stand in front of him. I fumble to my feet and walk to the point he commands. My feet move a shoulder width apart and one hand cups the other behind my back, eyes straight ahead.

"You're out of practice." It is a statement, not a question.

Silence hangs in the air and I fight the desire to move my body.

"You are here for confession. As such, after the confession I will deliver a penance to help you remove the obstacle between us. Normally, confession is an option, but you've already lied today."

A sigh escapes my lips, and I brace internally for his reaction.

"Normally, a Dominant would not be in this position, but your words today tell me you've relinquished your position through your actions. A true disappointment. Your job, in that position, is to protect, care, guide and provide an example for those who follow your lead. It can be a burdensome position, but when done right, it is rewarding beyond measure."

Each word punctuates my internal thoughts. I want to scream that there's an exceptionally good reason for my poor external actions. To tell him they were based in protection and not harm, but my lips remain firmly shut. He is correct.

Dominick walks around from the desk and moves to sit in the chair in front of me. Once he is seated, he makes the sign to kneel.

I fall to my knees and work to keep the painful posture.

"Shall we begin?" he asks and gives silent permission for my verbal response.

"As you wish, Sir."

He raises one eyebrow, but no other words or commands follow it. I know he expects me to fall into the ritual long ago established, but not one part of me wants to take part.

Dominick waits patiently for me to make the next move. Nothing in his manner is rushed or demanding. He waits until I am ready, knowing each moment of silence works on my need to express my apologies and explain why I am here.

I close my eyes and gather courage. When I open them, I begin to speak.

"On my knees before you, in humble submission, I come to you in an act of confession. In this place I seek your guidance, your firm hand and resolution of those things I hold internally, perpetrated or thought in a way which does not serve me, or my relationships, to be their best. Here, I seek absolution of my mistakes so I may grow from them. I give myself to you to provide a physical path to release these things." I chant the words I've not said in years but sit readily on my tongue. "My last confession was over five years ago."

"In this place I will provide the guidance as I see fit. Here I will offer you the forgiveness you seek, a path for repair, and the physical expression of resolution through pain and penance. To move forward, you must be willing and able to accept these paths without reservation or trespassing upon other relationships. Do you seek and offer these things?"

"I do," I state.

"Then let us start with why you lied about your reason for showing up in my class today."

SILENCE ENGULFS ME, BUT MY MIND RACES. MY RELATIONSHIP with Dominick was always tumultuous. While I originally came to him in the position of a submissive, it quickly turned into one of consensual slavery. In that place, I found a peace and contentment I've rarely duplicated. In every way he owned me, and I followed his lead.

In me he saw something I did not always see in myself. Through fire and persistence, he honed my skills as a top and taught me the other side of power exchange relationships. Each step created through exactness. A consistent repetition of skills until I did them with accuracy.

Over time, I took on clients as a professional. Sessions were always about command and control. The discipline of self and emotions held to a level to create a hard exterior and give the client a place of release. The men and women he introduced me to were often in powerful positions, which later served my ability to create the world I normally inhabited.

He always hated my duplicative desires. Our ultimate falling out came from my desire to appear "vanilla" to my family and the world. To be successful in that realm and prove I could be just as successful in the world I'd chosen to step into. Dominick's warning haunts my thoughts now.

"You can't live both at the same level. Something always gives, but if you try, make sure you always have a strong team around you. There are no secrets in life that time does not reveal. Always tread carefully."

I thought him to be an arrogant old fool and stormed out of his house. While we'd repaired the initial riff between us, I swore I'd never train others in his manner or harshness. I would show him I could do it all without him.

It is not lost on me as I kneel before him that my arrogance and over-confidence brought me here. Time did indeed reveal all my secrets.

"My worlds collided," I start, my voice a whisper. "A need I did not know still existed lulled me into a place of false security."

Dominick does not move. He does not speak. In his silence, I know I've not given him what he wants to know.

"I was dating a PR client's brother. She is in a contentious Congressional race. Someone in the press ran the plates to one of the vehicles to the 'wrong' persona. It quickly became headline news."

The words come out in a rush. Of all the reasons I walked away, this is the easiest one to explain, and I hope it will satisfy him.

"When the headlines read he was out with a professional Domi-natrix, the scandal was a typical DC explosion. At the time he and I were out, I was in my 'vanilla persona.' The pictures did not catch my face, but his was on full display. I wanted to help calm the situation by removing myself from it. I'm sure we've lost the client and others lost their positions on the campaign."

My head falls and I blink back tears. I can hear Reece's accusations and tone swirl with the weight of thoughts in my mind. My heart breaks all over again. Everything in me hopes the explanation is enough.

"How long ago did you leave, Atlas?"

Dominick's question is simple, and I feel the weight of his stare.

"Six weeks." The answer comes automatically from my lips.

When I finally center myself and look up, I know I've miscalculated my situation.

"Let me clarify my understanding. You walked out on a professional PR client, over a situation you created by your own lack of focus. You did not tell your business partner or your security lead, both of whom you've known and trusted for almost a decade?"

"Yes, Sir." I work to put confidence and steel in my voice.

"For six weeks you've not contacted them? They do not know where you are or if you are alive?"

His words shape the narrative in a way that makes me feel foolish. Without giving all the other situations in play, they make me sound like a weak fraud. None of them sound dominant, caring, leading or protective. It sounds like the break-up of a silly little girl who was only an imposter in the life I created.

"Yes, Sir."

They are the only words I allow to cross my lips. Any amount of pain or penance is worth it to keep everyone safe from Edmund's threats. When he'd first proposed, I thought it was an infatuation between a client and a professional, but it had escalated. He has the means to make good on every one and even worse if he chooses.

"Is that the sole reason you walked away?"

I press my lips together and refuse to acknowledge the question. To say anything would create a lie or expose him to possible harm. With a deep breath, I brace for my next words.

"In these things I confess and ask your guidance in redeeming the mind through the penance of the body to focus self. Your guiding hand gives me the strength to know excellence is not an accident. It results from high intention, sincere effort, and intelligent execution. Determining destiny by choice not by chance, through the wise choice of many alternatives. I give to you my willingness to take your council and follow the immediate path to find wisdom in my constant strive for such excellence."

The chant is both my execution and my salvation. In it, I end the need to confess further. By it, I hand over my immediate fate to Dominick, and all I can do is wait.

THE ONLY BREAK IN THE SILENCE IS MY SHALLOW BREATHS. My body aches. Still Dominick does not move or make a sound. Not wanting to see the disappointment in his eyes, my own stare at the floor between his feet.

"Forgiveness is not due you. There are things you aren't telling me. Still, you've come to me knowing my expectations. Seeking a haven in my abode and under my roof. Thus, punishment and penance are due for a tongue which will not confess. You will find the list of them, and the necessary supplies, in your room upon waking."

I sigh in a combination of dread and relief. All I need is time to figure out what I need to do next. It isn't the first time I've faced this situation, and in comparison it feels like the best option. I knew what I would face here, but I also knew I would be cared for and safe.

Dominick rises from his chair, and I lift my head enough to be able to see his hands. He moves around the desk and sits. Without another word, he hits a button on his phone and dials.

The dial tone slips into a ring and on the second ring is picked up.

"Good evening, The Empyrean Club. How may I help you this evening?" The voice comes across the speaker phone.

"Good evening. Thomas Kinkaid, please."

My head snaps up and I scramble to my feet.

"NO!" I scream. "You can't..."

In quick order, Dominick signals for silence and commands me to kneel. Automatically my body follows both and I fall to the floor. My heart races in a state of panic, but the look on his face tells me I am already pushing his patience.

"Kade." I hear the reply on the other end of the phone. Dominick picks up the receiver and presses a button on his phone.

"Thomas. It's Dominick. Yes, it has been quite a bit of time, boy... I'm sure you've been busy. It is okay... I understand why you've not kept in touch lately."

There's a long pause and I shake my head no, pleading silently with him.

"I see... It has come to my attention you might be a bit extra busy at the club as of late... Why didn't you tell me Atlas was missing?"

His tone is even and stern. A dark look crosses Dominick's face. I know I've placed Kade in this position and now he's going to face Dominick's ire because of me.

"Yes. Well, you and your team can rest easy, but I expected you to call in such a situation... Atlas is here... Just this afternoon....yes... showed up in my class... Did she? Samantha is faster than I remember then... She's fine... no, she's not hurt... No, tell Samantha to stay there... I don't know... no... I'll have someone from the household pick you up tomorrow...I understand, we'll expect you at Logan wheels down around 4:00p or so... I'll make your arrangements from here... No, I'm not happy with her either... Very good."

Dominick places the receiver back in the cradle.

"Whatever is going on with you, we're going to get to the bottom of it, even if I have to bring the world you carry on your shoulders crashing down around you. I trained you better than this and I expect more from you."

For the first time in weeks, a tendril of anger replaces the edge of fear. I walked away to protect my entire world, and no one is going to destroy it. With effort, I pull my shoulders back and stare hard back at Dominick.

A smile curls around the edges of his lips.

"About time you showed up, girl," he says. No amusement penetrates his tone.

"You are dismissed."

Without dropping my gaze, I stand and back out of the room. Once my feet touch the threshold, I turn on my heels and head back to my room.

CHAPTER THREE

SOFT LIGHT FILTERS through the windows. Under me, the pillow is damp from tears shed in the night until my body faded into the darkness of sleep. Scenes from the previous day skim across my mind. After six weeks of moving around the East Coast, my cash reserves are running low, and I need to find a way back without eliciting more action from Edmund.

I thought I could easily maneuver around Dominick in the safety of his household. Now I am not sure why I thought it would be so easy. Ego is such a dangerous thing, and he is as demanding as ever.

With a stretch, I sit up in the bed. My body aches from the lack of sleep and the unpracticed positions. With each passing minute, the room brightens with the rising sun. On the meditation mat in front of me sits a basket placed there sometime while I slept. I shudder at the possibilities running through my mind. Still, I reach out and pick up the envelope on top and slip the parchment paper from it.

My fingers tremble as it unfolds. With a deep breath, I focus on the words.

"Atlas, my disappointment knows no bounds in your current set of actions. Like a wayward child, you return to my world but unlike the

prodigal, you are not contrite or forthcoming. During your training, there were so many hopes and possibilities for your future but from my current perspective, you've squandered them all. I can only hope I am wrong."

The words are a punch in the gut. Dominick's violent disappointment in me is worse than any physical rituals he may place at my feet.

"In this basket lie the implements of your physical torment. As you desire to carry your burden without speaking, so will you suffer without direct witness; but do not think it is without notice. Your room, as you are aware, houses several small cameras to verify your ability to at least follow directions."

My hands shake. I almost want him to yell at me. Everything in me wants someone to hold me and show me a path to protect those I love so deeply, but it isn't offered because I do not ask for it. When I walked out, I knew it was to be a lonely road, but I did not imagine this harshness.

"Your uniform is now replaced with the enclosed sackcloth. May it remind you of the debasement you've brought on to yourself, a mourning of the lies and omissions which both cross and hold you in your own personal hell. May it give you a place to repent your violation of the basic tenants we hold most dear.

On your desk, you will find hardtack and water. It will give you sustenance but no enjoyment in its consumption.

Now for your penance. Let this be a time of reflection and understanding through the physical to release your mental hold.

Shackles: You will wear shackles on your ankles and wrists. Let them remind you that running away hobbles the ability of others to help in your darkest time of need. Once you lock them in place, as you've done by running away, there they will remain until someone else removes them.

Locked inside: This room is familiar to you, as you've spent much time in it. It is locked to ensure your whereabouts are known. For trust is hard to build and easy to violate, and you've destroyed it in many ways.

Chamberpot: Under the window sits a chamberpot for your use. As your actions were uncivilized, so shall your needs be met in a similar manner.

Bag of Rice: Finally, there is a bag of rice on which to kneel and contemplate the pain your actions have caused others. To avoid it will only mean more time to contemplate it. May it loosen your tongue, allow you to open and walk back into the fold of your chosen family. Today you will only have two choices of position. You may stand in your self-righteousness or kneel in the pain of your actions."

By the end of the note, tears stream down my face. Each accusation rings through me. My stomach rumbles. With an effort, I remove the uniform which stole my dominant position and replaced it with the sackcloth which lowers me further still.

———

THE SACKCLOTH RUBS HARSHLY AGAINST MY SKIN AS I PULL IT over my head. I walk over to the window's rising light. Outside, the world stirs. Below people jog down the sidewalks and cars rush past to carry people to their lives. In here, it feels as if my life has stopped. Both a prison and a refuge.

I turn toward the desk and grab the bag of rice on the way. This cloth bag is meant for this exact punishment. Its rough surface abrades the skin while the hard grains of rice poke and prod at the knees. I lower my body down onto it and pour a glass of water.

Several pieces of hardtack sit on a plate in front of me. When I lived here, we often made the substance traditionally, using water, flour and salt. Since it can sit for months without spoiling, it served two purpose—the first in the making, working with your hands and yet knowing a misstep would make it your only meal. Then in the eating. It is a slow process to break it apart or to wait for one to two hours for it to absorb water enough to eat without letting it completely dissolve. Both parts require a patience lost in today's hustle and bustle. Dominick was always good at teaching things in unexpected ways.

I gnaw on the hard cracker until it breaks apart. The process is slow and tedious. My knees scream with each move of my body as it rocks. Each bite is an effort. I drink a fast glass of water to help quell my hunger more quickly. Once my stomach settles, I place the remaining hardtack in the glass to soak in hopes of an easier meal later.

Finally, I walk back to the basket and lift the heavy iron shackles. The combination of physical weight and symbolism pushes me to the edge. I lift the first pair; I place each one around my ankles and lock them in place. The short connecting chain cuts my steps in half. Lifting the second pair, I repeat the process on my wrists. The short distance between my hands makes me struggle to lock them in place. Once done, I turn to rearrange my bed back to a couch.

Movement is a struggle. Each thing takes twice the effort.

In front of me is a long day. A rotation of standing with the weight of iron weighing on me or kneeling on the bag of rice.

Then there is the problem of Kade.

CHAPTER FOUR

SHADOWS once again cast across my small room. Soon all light will be lost. With the shackles on my limbs, I will be in a disadvantaged state to maneuver. I place the last piece of now softened hardtack on the plate. With a shuffle around the room, I arrange things to the smallest detail so I will remember them. When the last of the day's light disappears, I mourn its loss. Once again, I kneel on the rice and consume the tasteless meal. As the last bite hits my mouth, the locks on my door click.

Light from the hallway streams in and Ana once again appears at the entrance.

"Master requests the company of your presence in the library. I am told you know the way." Without further comment, she walks away.

I rise from the desk and shuffle like a prisoner through the hall-way. With care, I move down the stairway. Each step is a practice in focus. Both feet must meet the step before proceeding to the next one. It is a slow process.

As I approach the entrance to the living room, I can easily hear Dominick's and Kade's voices.

"I don't know what the hell she was thinking," Kade rages and I cringe.

"Boy, you either learn to control your temper under my roof or I will control it for you," Dominick replies.

"Yes, Sir. I'm frustrated. For weeks we've worried."

"I know." Dominick's tone softens. "She's hiding something, and I plan to get to the bottom of it."

"I don't understand why she didn't tell us. There's nothing we won't take on for her." Kade lets out an exasperated breath. "I can only hope this has nothing to do with Edmund."

"Who is Edmund?" Dominick queries.

At the sound of his name, I panic and move with a struggling quickness as I battle the shackles. Everything in me needs this line of questioning to end.

The clanking sound of my shackle chain banging on the floor makes both heads jerk up in my direction.

Shock blooms on Kade's face. Without a mirror, I can only imagine the poor sight I am to behold. I struggle into the room.

"Eavesdropping isn't any more becoming than lying, Atlas."

"Yes, Sir. I am sorry, Sir."

His hand makes the sign to kneel and points to the pillow in the floor. The small act of kindness allows hope to take root. My knees hit the pillow harder than expected and I wince in pain. Beside me I can hear Kade gasp.

"What the hell, Dominick!"

"Kade... don't." The whispered words force through my lips.

"How dare you debase her this way! She came to you for help and you want to break her more? Do you treat all Dominants this way or is this a game of humiliate the Dominant in front of a previous submissive? Are you kidding me, man?"

"Kade," Dominick growls as he steps beside me, his fingers snapping. "Sit. We can discuss this later. There are more pressing things right now."

I watch his feet stomp across the floor. Above me Dominick turns toward me.

"Atlas, the situation you created is obvious. Today you've paid penance. Shall we try your state of confession again?"

I nod as I struggle to form the words.

"Yes, Sir."

"Before we begin"—he turns toward Kade—"you will be silent through this ritual unless you are engaged to speak, boy. This course of action requires your respect of the participants and the ritual. If you cannot offer it, then I advise you to leave now."

"I'll stay." Kade's clipped words do nothing to settle my nerves.

Dominick sits in the chair next to Kade's and right in front of me. They are oppositional forces. Where Dominick's body is tall and fit like a swimmer, Kade is a bodybuilder who is built like a tank. With one, the dominance exudes in the air and the other is submissive but never lacks strength. Regardless, both are fiercely loyal and protective. If I were not the center of their ire, I would appreciate it.

The air in the room grows heavy as two pair of eyes bear down on me expectantly.

"On my knees before you, in humble submission, I come to you in an act of confession. In this place I seek your guidance, your firm hand, and resolution of those things I hold internally, perpetuated or thought in a way which does not serve me, or my relationships, to be their best. Here, I seek absolution of my mistakes so I may grow from them. I give myself to you to provide a physical path to release these things."

"Are you contrite, Atlas?"

"I am contrite, Sir."

"Tell me how you came to this state." Dominick's tone is hard, but there is an underlying kindness. Beside him, Kade shifts uncomfortably.

"Lessons are best taught through a tangible interpretation. In it, I know my actions appear selfish and weak. Rather than trusting those around me, I lifted the world alone and ran with it. In doing so, I left an unintentional wake of chaos and pain. Today, I faced this path through enduring physical pain, humiliation, restricted movement, and loneliness. Each one I brought on to myself and deserve to bear."

I hear Kade clear his throat and immediately I see Dominick's hand command him to silence before the words cross his lips. While I trained Kade, he had the rare occasion to submit to Dominick. The commands were the same no matter who produced them.

"Why are you here, Atlas?" Dominick inquires.

"I am exhausted. I am afraid. I am lost. I hurt beyond measure." The simple words are all I can produce. Each one is true but incomplete.

"Penance can produce all of those things."

"Those things were upon my shoulders when I crossed your threshold. Penance only forced me walk into them rather than run away from them."

"Tell me of your hurt, girl." The endearment cracks my lagging resolve.

"I hurt because I've hurt those I love dearly. In my haste to act and keep them safe, I broke the tenets of my life. The foundation in which I built my world."

"How are you lost?"

"I do not know the way forward. The wrong move is dangerous, and I no longer know the right ones."

"Why are you exhausted?" Dominick's voice is almost soft, but I know too much to fall into the trap of believing not moving forward will keep it that way.

"Because I'm running and I'm out of the energy to do so." My voice sounds tired, even to my own ears. I brace for the next question. He's listened to me dance around it over the last few. Even to my ears it is obvious, and I know he is leading me to the exact place he wants me to go.

The weight of their gaze sits on me as they both look down from above. There is no tenseness in Dominick's posture, while Kade looks ready to kill someone, and I don't know in this moment if it is me or the man beside him.

"Who is Edmund and why are you afraid of him? What makes him dangerous and why do you need to keep those around you safe from him?" The unexpected combination of questions stuns me into silence, and my brain works to form a set of half-truths. "And don't even think about lying to me, girl. Today was light, and you still owe payment when we are done with you."

A combination of fear and respect rips through me.

CHAPTER FIVE

THERE ARE no words for his questions. Beside him Kade sits up and watches me. My mind races. Each heartbeat reminds me of a threat he issued. I take a deep breath.

"Edmund is a professional client of Alexandra's." I try to keep my tone neutral as I utter my alter ego's name.

"Don't try my patience tonight," Dominick warns, and I look up.

Fury and pain cross Kade's face as he realizes he was right in his assessment, but too late to be able to act on it. Now those emotions are turned on me because I did not confide in him.

"He proposed after a session, several months ago. I rejected the proposal."

"This is not an unusual situation when an infatuation gets out of hand."

Dominick's comment goads me to go deeper with my explanation.

"True, but Edmund is... unique." I try to place the word delicately; not even I want to face the truth.

"Unique how?"

"He is possessive, arrogant, intelligent, obsessive, and that is before you know he can easily buy and sell a small country," Kade says with loathing.

Dominick cuts his eyes but does not reprimand the intrusion.

"All of those things are true to some degree," I confirm.

"Were you always afraid of this client?"

"No. In a scene, his manners are impeccable. He is thoughtful and polite. Exacting in following every order. Until..." I let the word hang as the memories haunt me.

Dominick sits in silence as I gather my thoughts. When seconds turn into minutes, he prompts, "Until when?"

"Until he stalked me." My voice is hoarse, forced across my vocal cords.

"Son of a bitch!" Kade swears under his breath. "I will kill that mother..."

"That's enough, Kade," Dominick reprimands before his tirade takes hold.

"Continue," he says to me.

"He wanted to own me. To keep me locked up in his world so he could pretend I was in control. I didn't realize the depth of his desire until I rejected him." I move my hands and the weight of the shackles pull on my shoulders. "Soon after, he threatened me. He taunted me with my security being close, leaving flowers in my offices with menacing notes. On the surface, it looked sweet, if a little obsessive, but the notes were callous."

A shudder rolls through me.

"You said offices. He left you notes in both the club and the PR office?" Dominick doesn't let the detail get missed.

I nod.

"Words." The command is simple.

"Yes. Flowers were left or delivered to both offices and both personas. He knew my secrets."

Kade shifts in his chair restlessly, but Dominick is steady throughout the explanation.

"When the situation with Reece's sister blew up, I knew Edmund was behind it." At my own mention of Reece's name, I fall forward on my hands. The words lay bare all the things I've held for weeks. My stomach rolls, and I am glad of its limited contents.

"In that moment, I realized I could not keep my family safe and my only option was to get as far away as possible. Reece discovered my secrets in the process since he was out with Atlas at the time of the picture. Now he hates me. Edmund wants to possess me and will ruin everyone around me to get to me. With so much in ruins, I ran. I want everyone safe. It is the only thing I could do. Instead, I've lost everything I ever built or loved to a madman."

"What about you, Atlas? Are you not important in this scenario?" Dominick finally asks.

"It is why I left everything behind on my desk and took cash. I thought if I could just get away for a few weeks it would all settle down. In the meantime, it seemed intelligent to be as untraceable as possible."

From the corner of my eye, I see Kade's anger increase.

With a nod from Dominick, Kade turns toward me. I brace for the tidal wave of emotions.

"How dare you!" Kade growls. "Do you think so little of me? Or the team I've built? Do you not think me capable of keeping you AND your secrets safe?"

"It's not like that, Kade. Please understand, all I wanted to do was keep everyone safe," I plead.

"Safe? You call this safe? Edmund is running around your club. The man you accuse of stalking. Interacting with every single member in the place. How the hell do you call THAT keeping everyone safe?"

I shake my head. "I didn't think he was a threat to the membership. He hasn't..." The words won't form in my mouth.

"No. He's as cordial as always, other than he's at the club more than normal. He asks about you often, but we thought it was a client thing." He works to control the volume of his voice, but I know him. The hold is tenuous.

"Then it looks like my removal from the situation created a temporary solution."

I lift my eyes and glare at him.

"If you'd come to your SECURITY team, we wouldn't have a situation which needed a temporary solution," he screams.

"Well, if I thought you could control someone with more money than the GDP of a country without getting hurt, I would have told you," I yell back.

Kade jumps to his feet and looms over me. I refuse to shrink even when his huge frame casts a shadow.

"You don't think I can keep you safe? I would lay my life down for you, Atlas! You are the most important person in the world. Yet you don't trust me with your life! How dare you! Your actions are foolish, selfish, and stupid. The mess you've left in your wake is much harder to contain. I've assembled the best team available and your actions tell us we suck!" Kade roars.

I am taken aback by the ferocity of his words. They make me feel foolish, selfish, and stupid. In those moments of immediate fear, all I could see was harm to Samantha, Kade, or Reece. There were not thoughts past those. The threats are real, and I knew it.

"I know you would die trying to protect me, and it scares me more than anything else," I state.

Kade paces beside me. Each step vents more of his anger. The knowledge I've sent him to his knees with a simple command and the fact he cares so deeply for me is the only reason I know his anger isn't directed at me but his feeling of helplessness.

"So one man wants to make you his prisoner, and another puts you willingly in chains. It's like I know nothing about you. And you call yourself a Dominant?" The last sentence is like a slap in the face. It steps too far over the line, and I will not abide it.

"No man put her in chains, Kade," Dominick states with a calmness which sits dichotomously in the situation playing out before him.

"Really, Dominick? She kneels on the floor in shackles in your home. You can't tell me she did this to herself!" Kade turns toward the other man.

"It is exactly what I am telling you," he replies.

"What the hell is going on here?"

"If you will sit down and find control, Kade, you will see."

Above me, he continues to pace.

"Thomas Kinkade, the actions here are my own. There is a gym down the street when we are done here. Now sit." I pull on the last bit of my reserves to issue the command with strength.

"You are in no position..." he starts.

"Do you believe a Dominant on their knees is less respectable than a submissive in the same place?" Dominick interjects.

"Yes, because there is no such thing as a Dominant who kneels."

"Then you are a fool, and I do not suffer such well. Now sit. We will discuss your actions and words shortly."

"I do not need you to fight my battles," I growl.

Dominick's head whips around.

"I note your continued lack of humility, girl." The underlying kindness in his tone is gone.

"Now, if you two are done being children, shall we solve this mess?"

"Kade, your vehement expression of Atlas' position surprises me and runs counter to the training I thought you received. Maybe you also need a lesson in humility, but it will need to wait for another day," Dominick says to Kade and motions him to the chair next to him.

Kade pauses. An audible sigh escapes him. Then he nods his head in deference and returns to his seat.

"Please accept my humble apologies for my lack of control... Sir."

"You know the expectation, Kade, and the price."

Kade nods.

"As far as a Dominant on their knees—they lose nothing through submission. In my house, I use penance and corporal mortification to clear the mind and calm a person to create a greater self-awareness. A way to assuage emotions, battle their own internal demons, and pay for their slights against another human. Atlas was trained in this way. It matters not the fact she is dominant. She is human. In so, the emotions and tubulations she feels are powerful forces, as are those of all humans. This is a way to expel them from her own den of inner demons, battle them, and rid them from her world."

"I've never seen this or heard her say anything about it. She didn't train me this way," Kade spits.

"Respect, boy. You will show it or I will dismiss you from my household," Dominick warns.

"This ritual is paramount to being sacred, though I am surprised to hear she did not train you in the same way. Ultimately, the fault for that is on me." Dominick exhales, then continues. "It is not for show. This interaction is private. It humbles, give a place for open obedience and submission. You must understand the privilege you are allowed in being here. If you were not important to her, this would not be happening."

"Why in the world would a Dominant ever submit? Doesn't it go against the concept of dominance?" Kade sighs and looks down at me. It is softer but clearly confused.

"Dominance and submission are but a hair's breadth away, one from the other. Everyone submits to someone. How this is fulfilled differs from one person to another. Someone unable to be in a humbled position is not a person of strength and to submit is not one of weakness. Neither does it make them any higher or lower to do so. A person's 'status' is based on the person's interactions with others."

"You said she did this to herself."

Dominick nods.

"It is her penance. She comes to confess. To relieve the burdens she carries. In return, I give her a way to clear her own path and physically pay for the errors of her ways. The results of each penance she's endured so far, she did to herself—alone. Isn't that right, girl?"

CHAPTER SIX

BOTH SETS OF EYES TURN.

"Yes, Sir." I nod, sitting up straighter.

"Explain to your former submissive why you are here."

I shift on my knees. The bruises from the rice bloom in pain, while the weights of the shackles and the friction points they've worn also make themselves known. Kade and I've shared so much, but this secret feels almost too personal.

"The world is too heavy," I state. A fact I did not fully realize until I uttered it. "Contrary to my name, or because of it, there are times I need to put the world down. I take responsibility for things at every turn and in my secrets, I am alone. Many people know parts, but no one knows all. In this place, I can set it down. I am safe and taken to task for my faults. It may sound like an oxymoron, but it is what I know and what I need. For weeks, I wandered alone. The longer I did, the more guilt I felt until I no longer knew how to get back home. So I came to the only place that made sense."

"But I'm always by your side, Atlas. You've got me and Samantha." The hurt in Kade's voice nearly breaks me.

"You are both amazing, but look what happened. I blew it.

Samantha stepped away. She needs to spread her wings. You were focused on keeping the club safe. Besides, you both deserve to focus on your own lives. I am responsible for my world. The success of the PR firm, the club, my book sales. The list feels endless, but it is my job, and I wouldn't trade it. But one major threat and look at me, I suddenly cannot cope," I confess.

"It would take anyone sideways." Kade's voice works to soothe.

"What about Reece?" Dominick inserts into the conversation.

"What about him, Sir? He's gone and I can't imagine he'll breathe my name, outside a curse, for a long time."

"That's not true," Kade says. "He's worried sick about you. Blaming himself for pushing you away and exploding in your office."

"Do you love him, Atlas?" Dominick asks.

Flashes of our time together filter across my mind, and I smile. It is the first genuine one in weeks.

"I believed it to be possible," I reply without commitment. "He may not return the feeling. To be in that position of my life is a hard task; I do not wish it upon anyone."

"Where do we go from here?" Kade asks out loud.

"Shall we continue your confession, girl?"

"Yes, Sir."

"How long has it been since your last true confession?" Dominick asks, ending all other discussion.

"Five years, Sir, for even in my last attempt I did not confess from a point of contrition."

"Shall we begin?"

FOR THE NEXT HOUR, I CONFESS MY 'SINS' AND FEARS. AMONG them sit my dishonesty by an omission in entering Dominick's house and lack of training Kade fully in our tradition. I pour out the fear which made me run, and the threats made against everyone I loved. In the end, I am kneeling before them both, drained.

"I believe that is enough for one evening," Dominick finally says.

"In these things I confess and ask you guidance in redeeming the mind through the penance of the body to focus self. Your guiding hand gives me the strength to know excellence is not an accident. It results from high intention, sincere effort, and intelligent execution. Determining destiny by choice not by chance, through the wise choice of many alternatives. I give to you my willingness to take your council and follow the immediate path to find wisdom in my constant strive for such excellence," I chant.

"Do you seek and accept the penance offered by those you kneel before?" Dominick asks.

"I do."

"Your penance will serve as a reminder that inward pain causes outward pain to others when you hide yourself. To this end, you will suffer for your many omissions and lies which violate the foundational trust of every power exchange relationship you've held, both personally and professionally. It is a thing to keep the secrets of self, it is another to create a situation where a lack of information can cause irreparable damage and take the decisions from those who would have free will. You are found wanting and lacking in these areas," Dominick pronounces.

"Tonight, your body will pay for that which your mind withheld. Each count will mark upon you a reminder of the very foundation of your world. It will shore up the cracks and offer a road to repair. In addition, it will help complete the training of our tradition which you failed to impart."

I watch Dominick walk across the room. He opens the lock on a cabinet near the wall and removes something from it. As he walks back, my eyes drop to the object in his hand. The intake of air is pure fear. The black whip uncurls when he releases his fingers.

"I presume you know how to use one of these," he says, handing it to Kade.

"Yes, but..." Kade starts.

"There's a target on the wall to the left. Please show me."

Kade flicks his wrist and the tip of the whip lands on the bulls-eye.

"Very good." Dominick nods and turns to me.

"Your penance is fifty strikes, which Kade will deliver. His failure to do so in an appropriate manner will ensure the number is doubled and I will deliver the second one. Am I clear?"

"Yes, Sir." Our voices chime in unison but I cannot meet Kade's eyes.

No one speaks as we make our way to Dominick's room of torment. A place where punishment and pleasure are carried out for the beauty of pleasure mixed with pain to create a mutual satisfaction.

In front of me, the short single tail whip swings loosely at Kade's side. Many times before, the whip swung from my hand as I prepared to give Kade what he needed to release his own demons.

When we enter the room, the sound of shackle chains bounce off the walls.

"Kneel in front of the whipping post, girl," Dominick's voice commands from behind me.

I shuffle to the piece of equipment and struggle to kneel without help. Once in position, Dominick binds my ankles to the stand. The rough sackcloth lifts over my head and hangs limply around my wrists. Wrist shackles are pulled through the neck hole and fastened to the post. In every way I am exposed.

Before I catch my breath, the tail of the whip bites against my skin. It takes everything I have not to scream. Every muscle tenses in revolution. I will my body to relax, but it refuses.

"Breathe, Atlas," Kade coaches behind me, his tone confident and even. The irony of our reversed positions adds to the intensity of the situation.

I breathe in. The next strike punishes my back and I bite back the scream.

"Relax into it," he says with more command but doesn't let up on the strikes.

Each one is timed to let the sharpness of the pain barely dissipate before the next one marks its place on my skin.

My fingers ball up and flex to give me something on which to focus. Sweat forms across my body.

"You need to give in to it. Let it take you down. Feed all of your sins to the pain." I hear him behind me.

So many times I've watched as he's taken the strikes from my whip, I never imagined I'd be in this position.

No two strikes are in the same place. They do not stray high or low.

The next one streaks across my back and slices the flesh. I scream. The only result is an increase in ferocity and focus. Kade no longer lets me collect myself after each one.

They land in quick succession. Tears roll down my face.

I rock my body to lessen pain by the smallest increments, but it doesn't help. Muscles across my body twitch and flex.

The harshness of the lashes makes me pull toward the post.

"I can't..." I pant.

"You can and you will," Dominick says from behind me.

Next to my ear the whip cracks and I jump at the sound.

"Focus. Breathe through each one. Relax your body." Kade's words are steel, yet each one is laced with a calm, steady care.

My mind races against the onslaught.

More strikes rain down on me, and I lose count. Screams and sobs echo off the walls as my body pays the price for my confession. There is nothing stoic about my penance. Emotions rush forward, expressing themselves in the agony.

My body sags against the post, no longer able to hold itself upright. Acceptance takes hold, and my body releases its own relief.

The last strikes lash against my body. A shudder releases my held breath.

Hands disconnect the shackles from the post. My head touches the floor. Sobs rock through me until they turn to a rain of tears. When there's nothing left to give, hands work on my back.

Salve is pressed into the wounds I know are present. A large bandage is applied over the area. The sackcloth lowers back into place.

Two chairs are pulled in front of me. Kade and Dominick take their respective places.

I work to control my breath. My muscles tense as I pull myself up. A hiss counteracts the pain of each movement.

On my hands and knees, I push forward. Pins and needles stab at my legs and feet as the circulation returns. With an effort, I crawl to Kade's feet.

My head lifts to look up until my eyes meet his. It is impossible to look away from his hard gaze.

"Head down," Kade commands.

"As you've come before us, contrite in your desire to seek reparations for your 'sins,' know you are forgiven. Now, properly thank Kade for his attention in this matter."

My head bends until my lips are right above the toe of his boot. There they hover as I wait.

"You must give her permission," Dominick prompts.

The harsh intake of breath from Kade rushes a thousand thoughts through me. I count my breaths to hold myself steady. As I approach a hundred, I hear his voice above me.

"You may." His voice is firm.

"Thank you," I whisper.

My lips brush the edge of each of Kade's boots without marring the high shine. Then I maneuver my body to repeat the process for Dominick.

"You are not yet worthy," I hear him say above me. The simple words rip through me in a way the pain of the whip could never do. I crawl back until my forehead touches the floor.

"Thank you for your council, time, focus, and consideration in this my confession," I say into the carpet below me.

"Do you believe her confession has relieved her of the shackles upon her inner mind enough to relieve her outer body?" I hear Dominick ask Kade.

"I believe she's paid a high enough price," Kade replies, his voice unsure.

"That is not the question. Do you think she's learned from her penance?"

"I do."

"Then, if you choose, you may release her from the weight of her own bondage."

Above me, I hear the rattle of keys.

"Kneel up," Kade commands. The shackles on my wrists fall away.

CHAPTER SEVEN

THE MORNING LIGHT casts a line across my eyes, and I blink against the assault. I stretch and immediately regret it. Pain shoots through the muscles in my back and the skin stretches across the wounds. My body aches from sleeping in a limited position. A moan escapes my lips to release the tension. With an effort, I swing my legs over the bed.

There is no breakfast on my desk. At the thought my stomach growls and begs for anything to help it settle. Even unshackled, my body is feeble in its attempt to move. I shuffle to the desk for water. The cool liquid is exquisite on my tongue. With greed I drink it down in large gulps.

Locks on the doors click and I jump at the sound. The movement causes the whip marks to ignite.

Ana walks into the room. She dashes my hopes for a reprieve on food when I realize her hands are empty.

"Master says it is time for you to purify yourself. I prepared an Epsom salt bath for you. Please follow me," she says and turns down the hall.

Her words penetrate my mind and an audible groan slips

between my lips. While the Epsom salt bath will soothe the aching muscles, the payment will lace pain when the water hits the open wounds.

I gather myself and follow Ana down the hallway.

We turn and walk into the large guest bathroom. Dominick was always fond of being able to play or give discipline wherever and whenever it was deemed necessary. Every bathroom in the house is equipped and sized appropriately.

The large soaking tub emits columns of steam. My muscles tense at the soothing concept but stop short in anticipation of the payment.

Ana reaches over to help me remove the sackcloth. Then she pulls on the edge of the bandage and removes it.

For a long moment, I stare at the bath.

Beside me, I hear Ana give an exasperated sigh.

"It seems I am not the only one who needs to learn patience and humility," I comment as I sit on the edge of the tub and swing my legs into the water.

"I don't even understand why you are here," she says openly.

"Careful, girl, I am still a guest and a Dominant in this household." My voice is monotone without emotion or inflection.

With care, I lower my body into the water and let out a hiss as the Epsom saltwater works its way up my back.

"Based on what I've seen, I think you are deluding yourself. Master would never treat another Dominant like he's treating you." Her free conversation confirms the fact that she sees me as an equal or subordinate.

"You've much to learn," I comment. Everything in me fights against the pain. With care, I wash my body with handmade soap. It is a luxury I've not enjoyed for the past several months. Even with the discomfort, being able to take time to stop is a relief all its own.

"Obviously not from you," she says and rolls her eyes.

"I'll remind you of that one day," I reply and sink down into the water.

My body retaliates from the bath in some ways, while in others, tension I did not know I carried is melted away. Once the bath is complete, I shower to wash my hair and rinse away the dredges of my penance.

Drops pound across my face and chest as I move to keep the rain of water off my back. After nearly drowning myself twice, I finally finish washing and conditioning my hair. When the water turns off, Ana magically appears.

"Please sit." Her voice is kinder. The look in her eyes is pure confusion. I want to smirk. Instead I let my eyes cast down in false submission and sit at the vanity.

Behind me, Ana works on styling my hair. The sound of the dryer lulls against my senses. My mind is an odd dichotomy of pushing against the events of the last several days and relaxing into the expert hands behind me. With an effort, I close my eyes and give in to the moment.

Time passes without thought until pain streaks around my head. My eyes spring open. Ana presses the next thorned rose into the elegant updo.

"Master insisted. He says to remind you it is not complete." Concern laces her voice.

Unadulterated fear runs through me.

"Are you okay?" Ana asks. A look of confusion shadows her face.

I force a smile.

"Yes, Ana. The hairstyle is beautiful."

Behind me she gives a slight nod and I note the respect in the gesture.

It is then I realize Dominick knew of our earlier interaction and interjected to correct it at some point.

"Master requests you wear the dress he's provided for you." She motions over toward the door.

The long white dress, in a Grecian style, hangs over the back of the door. Its formality looks out of place, but upon closer inspection the fabric is thin, though it contains several layers.

I prepare to feel the fabric scrape across my back. When I turn it around, I realize it plummets to right above my ass. The entirety of every wound, bruise, and whip mark is on display.

Slipping into the dress is easy. The front cleavage point mimics the back. The dress covers and uncovers in the same breath.

"Please come with me to your room. There you will remain until you are summoned. There are no meals planned for you today. Water is provided to you," she says and leads me back to my room.

CHAPTER EIGHT

DAY FINALLY FADES INTO NIGHT. Boredom, hunger, and pain mix with the beauty and elegance I present. In the afternoon, Ana returned to my room and did my makeup. No words were spoken as she worked in a clinical manner.

Darkness threatens to overtake the light in my room, and as I prepare to plunge into the night, a knock on the door draws my attention and I open it out of habit. It opens without effort. Confusion overtakes me as I wonder why I sit in this room when leaving is an option, even if it was unknown. My mind spins on the problem.

In front of me, Kade clears his throat.

"Dominick told me about tonight," he starts. "You don't need to go through this, you know. We can end it all right here and call it good."

I shake my head. "I need to finish it."

"No, you don't. My demons are bigger than yours. This is insane, don't you think?"

"No. It needs to be done. To understand the tradition upon which I am built, you must understand the path before me."

Kade sighs. "Why did you not teach me in this manner?" His voice sits in a sad tone.

"When I was training you, I struggled to understand the dominant side of our tradition. Why there was a need for such rituals, penance, and disciplines. In some ways, they feel paramount to abuse, but it is the underlying connection which makes them so powerful for every person who is involved. Now I realize they heal in a way that doesn't happen in most relationships. Each thing resonates with the primal needs of a person. Religions were built on similar concepts. Our tradition came out of an old priesthood which believed pain and ecstasy cleanses the body and clears a path for growth," I explain. All the teachings of Dominick seem clearer than ever before.

The sound of our breaths fill up the space.

Finally, Kade nods.

He turns and escorts me down the stairs to my fate. Each step bounces the ring of thorns against my scalp and I wince in pain.

When we reach the library, Kade turns to Dominick.

"Be merciful," he starts. "I can vouch on her behalf. She is truly contrite for her disgraces. May the love and strength of her chosen family bring her solace in this, her deepest time of need. May this path give her a way to find amends to you, your House, your traditions, and herself. In the fullness of her confession, may you extend your forgiveness for her transgressions."

When he finishes, Kade bows to Dominick and takes his place beside him.

"Atlas, you seek comfort in your chosen family. In times of loneliness or doubt, seek their counsel to find a better path. When we allow others into our world, we can lift, enlighten and comfort one another through our turmoils and struggles. Yet you bear this burden alone and must thus pay the price alone. Strip and begin the long road to forgiveness." Dominick's voice is calm.

With an effort disproportionate to the task, the dress drops to the floor. I feign a confidence I do not know and work to push away the fear.

"Shall we begin?" Dominick asks.

Behind me I hear an intake of breath.

"What the hell is going on here?" Reece growls.

———————

THE SHOCK OF HEARING REECE'S VOICE RUNS THROUGH ME. A combination of anger, fear, and excitement compete to take root as I work to focus my emotion. I struggle to face forward and not spin on my heels to meet his gaze.

In front of me, Dominick nods and silently signals me to kneel. I sink to my knees. My eyes fall so I don't have to look into his eyes. Emotions rush through me.

This quiet communication tells me he knows I can fight my own battles but is taking this one for me. Part of me wants to be grateful and the other part wants to petulantly tell him I can do it myself. There's no way to face the path in front of me and the oncoming storm raging behind me. The choice is mine to follow now for strength later.

Both Kade and Dominick rise. They step around me to create a wall between Reece and me.

Still, I brace. The scene Reece walked into can be construed in so many ways. In it, I lack the knowledge of what information they gave him while they sequestered me. This puts me at a significant disadvantage, and I fight to remain still.

"Welcome to my home, Mr. Gabriel. It was a pleasure to speak with you earlier," Dominick says politely.

"Let me repeat my question. What the hell is going on here? You told me you knew Atlas' location, and that she was in trouble. Yet I arrive to find her naked and covered in marks. It doesn't look like she's in any trouble she didn't beg for." Reece's voice wavers between concern and anger.

"Not everything in life is as it appears on the surface."

Dominick's controlled voice holds an edge of authority. "This is the case before you."

"Let me talk to Atlas," Reece demands.

"Reece, she's fine, man." Kade jumps into the conversation. "Let's go in another room. I'll explain everything. It will make more sense if you let me fill in the blanks."

Tension rips through the room. Everyone holds a collective breath.

"Fine." Reece finally relents. "But it better be a damn good explanation."

"It is," Kade confirms. "You need to have an open mind. Have I steered you wrong over the past few weeks?"

"No." Reece sighs.

I exhale a deep breath. His presence brings with it a peace I did not know I missed. Guilt in leaving him washes over me.

Behind me footsteps move and fade.

"Shall we begin the long road, girl?" Dominick's voice startles me out of my rolling emotions.

"Yes, Sir."

———————

"DEATH MUST COME TO OUR EGO SO WE MIGHT ARISE AGAIN. Tonight, you will bear them all so in its death, you may find life," Dominick says solemnly.

He walks over to pick up a bamboo pole from the wall and lays it across my shoulders. My hands drape naturally across it. He binds them in place.

"The weight of our transgressions weigh upon us as we walk through this world. Releasing this weight allows us to be free to live and love without unnecessary turmoil. Unfortunately, few bear the necessary burden to find freedom. Do you acknowledge your failings?"

"I do."

"Do you choose to die in self, so you may once again rise to contribute to our world?"

"I do."

"As your confessor, it is my duty to pass judgment. I hereby find you guilty of condemning others to suffering and alienation through your indifference and anger. In this I find you guilty."

"Please have mercy on me." I say the words, but everything in me wants to run.

To the right side of the pole, Dominick adds a weight and I struggle against it to balance the pole on my shoulders.

"Do you accept the burdens and responsibilities of the life you've chosen and thus willing to bear the physical manifestation of these burdens?"

"I do."

He adds weights to the left side of the pole. For a moment, I am glad of the balance, but the additional weight soon pushes me down.

"The weight of your transgressions not only adds to your burden in life but also adds to the burden of those around you. In your attempt to present perfection, you've hidden your failures and fears from those who would be best able to help you through these times. Failure is part of the human experience, thus you must now bear the weight of these transgressions. Do you accept them?"

"I do."

Dominick adds heavy weights to both sides of the bamboo pole, and I struggle to stand under them.

"Are you willing to face those whom you've transgressed against?"

"I am." My words require effort to push out on a breath due to the weight of the bamboo pole.

Dominick stands in front of me as I struggle.

"You are here, Atlas, because you took these things upon you without thought to the wants, needs, and desires around you. In this,

I find you guilty and wanting," Dominick pronounces. "You've disgraced our traditions, your teachings, and the path you chose in life. For these transgressions you will pay with the pain you've caused others."

Tears press against my eyes, but I refuse to let them fall.

"Let us proceed."

CHAPTER NINE

DOMINICK STEPS in front of me. I follow without question.

My eyes focus on the ground. The weight of the bamboo rod sits on my shoulders and I stumble. With an effort, I catch myself in the next step, managing to stay upright.

Each step is slow. The bamboo rod rubs against the whip's abrasions. A groan sits right behind my lips.

Reece steps out of a room to my right. His sudden appearance causes my focus to shift. I trip over the edge of the hallway carpet. My body braces to slam against the floor but the impact does not come.

Behind me, the bamboo rod pulls back and my body is set upright.

"One must willing accept the help of others in humility and gratitude without resentment towards them or self." Kade's voice chants the words behind me.

"I am humbled by your assistance and thank you for being there in my time of need," I respond. The words grind deep. When Dominick first explained this path, I did not appreciate the level of significance each step represented. Now I feel foolish and grateful for the lessons in front of me.

"It is I who is humbled and in awe of your very existence, Atlas," Kade says behind me.

The tears which have long threatened to fall roll freely down my cheeks.

With a slow effort, I work my way down the hall toward Dominick's room of torment. I refuse to make eye contact with Reece as I pass. I cannot handle his disappointment or disgust in my predicament and ordeal.

When I approach the door, Dominick appears in front of me.

"Upon you, the burdens you bear are by choice. Here you will find their final resting place." His fingers work to untie my binds. Relief rolls in waves when the bamboo pole lifts from my shoulders.

I fall to my knees.

"Please have mercy upon me," I beg.

"Mercy is not due you," Dominick replies. "Be strong and bear your cross."

I do not want to move. Pain, emotions, and exhaustion war across my body. There is nothing left to give to the ravenous penance in front of me.

"Atlas." Reece's voice cuts through my internal refusals. "Do what must be done." There is uncertainty in his voice. I understand this confusion. For years I did not understand this type of ritual.

"No matter what—I am here." Pain and compassion lace his words.

Kade offers his hand. I take it, and he helps me to my feet.

I make my way to the Saint Andrew's cross. My legs and arms spread to the appropriate position in resignation. Around me hands make quick work of binding me in place.

"Life is about choices. Each choice impacts us and those around us. Life is about pain. In that pain we find a path which leads us toward the direction in which we need to go. Your current path is selfish and focused on the wrong things." Dominick's voice is resolute and without question.

"Forgive me, for I know not the path needed to resolve my transgressions." I force the words across my lips in reply.

"In front of you stands your creator, your redeemer and your sustainer. In this place you will become whole. As a combination, we are your creation, destruction, and preservation. Each of us will always play a significant role in your life. One where you will find a place of teaching, a place of enlightenment, and a place where you can both lead and follow." Dominick's words cut through me. They are deeper in meaning than anything I've faced before. Trepidation and fear consume me. "Many times throughout our lives we experience birth, life, and death. Today, you die."

Silence engulfs the room. No one speaks. A thousand thoughts run through my mind. Each one debates the metaphorical concept and the physical reality, unable to distinguish one from the other.

"Do you appreciate the life given to you or are you bitter with envy of the world around you? Desiring the things of others in the belief your path gives you not what you want or need, regardless of your success or the fact you are surrounded with family and love?"

"I do not appreciate all I have, my creator. I am bitter about the work I face on a daily basis and the many faces I must wear to appease others. The path upon which I walk feels weighty and unfair," I whisper. The words are right even if they are foreign on the tongue.

"I see." Dominick replies to my confession. He places four clothes pins, connected by a string, across my chest.

I groan against the pain.

"Are there areas where you hold back and in doing so fail to serve others and self?"

"Yes. There are many areas of self I hold in reserve. Upon me please have mercy for my stubbornness," I plead.

"Mercy is not due you," Dominick says and places four more clothespins across my skin.

"Do you appreciate the people around you and the support they provide?"

"I do not."

The words earn more clothespins.

Time stands still. After twenty, I lose count. It is like I am floating away from the scene. Still the questions come. Each one creates an answer which is only satisfied by more clothespins down my body.

The sting of a whip tail pulls my focus back from the floating space.

"You do not deserve to remove yourself from this situation." Dominick's voice cuts through the air.

"When all seems lost, are you willing to do whatever it takes to find the path home?"

The questions slam against my tattered emotions.

"Yes!" I declare without question.

"Good girl." Dominick's praise renews my strength. "The one hundred and eight clothespins resulted from your confession and the penitence to see you to the other side. Each person here is a witness to your confessions and sins. We are your justice, your redemption, and your mercy. Give me your final confession and let us bring the nasty business to an end."

The clothespins pinch and burn across every part of my body. They run from my chest to my legs. In some areas I am thankfully numb while others create a pain difficult to bear. My body shakes under the strain of the long ordeal.

"It's okay, Atlas. It's almost over. Just confess to us and let us expose your pain," Kade says next to my ear.

"Before you I confess my failure through my faults and missteps." The words are hard, and I struggle to form them. "In my thoughts, words and deeds I've failed you and ask for your mercy and forgiveness. Guide me to the right path."

In front of me, Dominick turns to Reece.

"Remove her pain and become her sustainer. The person she relies upon during both the good and bad times of life. A place where she finds solace and the one who can return her to all of us, should it be needed in the future."

He hands Reece the end of the cord. In that moment I realize the one hundred and eight clothespins are 'release' to my sins and may come off one at a time or in a single pull. Before me, Reece stands as my executioner.

CHAPTER TEN

THE WORLD around me is quiet. A thousand things run through my mind as I stare into his beautiful face. I drop my head and close my eyes to shut him out. Visions of being held in his arms, the picnic by the river or his lips on mine. Each one turns to the pain I saw in his eyes as he roared at me. The newspaper article plastering us across the top, proclaiming it as the Capitol area's most recent scandal. The situation that ripped another thing from my life and plummeted the knife deep into my heart. Past pains were so much easier to move past, but Reece touched too deep. He didn't just have the power to hurt me but to destroy the very essence of my soul. If I were to be honest with myself, it might be the love that poets and songwriters sing about or it could be the end of my world.

Reece flicks the whip and it bites into the side of my hip with a perfect stroke. My eyes spring open and I gaze at his beautiful face. He gives nothing away, but he keeps his eyes on mine. He doesn't blink. Everything about him is breathtaking. In such a short time, he's become important to my world.

"I'm sorry," I whisper.

He closes his eyes and exhales. "Why are you sorry?" He opens his eyes and looks at me puzzled.

"For everything."

"You need to be more specific, Atlas—or is it Alexandra?" His fingers remove the first clothespin. The blood rushes back into the skin. Pain washes across my body and mingles with the dull constant ache. I want to beg him to release them all at once and end this torture.

My head hangs. The effort and pain of my position causes my breaths to come in pants.

"I'm sorry." My voice is barely a whisper.

"It's not that easy," Reece replies. The look in his eyes runs between hard and gentle. "Your lie almost cost people everything they've worked for in life."

"I didn't lie." The words come out in a groan.

"Omission is a lie," he states.

"It's omission. A lack of information. There are things..." The words die on my lips. Edmund's threats flood my mind and I visibly shudder.

"There are things you do not tell others and thus cause pain. Yes. A lie by omission." Disappointment laces his tone. It hits me like a smack across the face.

"Please," I beg.

"Please what? Pull this string and let it end?" Reece brings the string taut.

I nod.

"You don't think you deserve pain at my hand?" The edge to his voice frightens me.

"Mr. Gabriel, if I can't trust you to carry out the position I've given you in this ritual with grace and mercy, I can dismiss you. This isn't about vengeance, malice or some displaced righteousness. It is about penance, forgiveness, and a way forward to heal the wrongs you've both created." Dominick's voice cuts through our exchange.

Reece's head snaps to the left. The tension in the room is palpable. I hold my breath. The silent battle wages in front of me. Pain laces through my body as the pinch of each clothespin torments my skin.

When Reece's head dips in silent acknowledgement, I exhale.

"Please forgive me for my transgressions." My eyes plead as I beg Reece for his forgiveness.

"I forgive you."

Reece pulls hard on the cord. In a single pull, the line of clothespins rips off my skin. Pain screams in the burning path. A scream rips through my throat. I howl in agony. Blood floods back to the numb skin and creates wave after wave of pain.

Hands take me down from the cross. A blanket wraps around my form as I am moved to the floor. Thoughts refuse to form. Pain pulses through me and I rock my body on my knees trying to process the words, pain, and emotions. Tears gather in the corner of my eyes. Something in me breaks open. The first sob escapes my lips. A torrent of tears follows. Pent-up emotions release in an unstoppable flood.

Time stands still. The pain slowly fades and morphs through my body until it is a dull ache. Exhaustion seeps through me. My eyes refuse to focus. Sobs wrack my body until they are hiccups. Each breath is barely a pant. A hand runs through my hair in a soft, soothing rhythm. Beside me, a low baritone voice encourages me.

"Breathe. Deep breaths. In and out. You're safe. It's over," he says in a never-ending loop. "You are so amazing."

My brain is fuzzy and light. Emotions form and dissipate with each breath. There's a comfort in this mental space. The hiccups slow. Each breath moves deeper, slower, longer. An arm pulls on my shoulder until I give in and fall sideways. My body stops before it hits the ground. My head lies on something soft. The hand continues to move through my hair. Breaths come in stuttered release. I relax into the constant rhythm across my head.

"Shh... It's okay. It's over," his voice continues.

My eyes close in relief. The last tension in my muscles lets go. Sleep pulls on me.

Somewhere a phone rings.

"Kade," a disembodied voice says. I cringed at the harsh intrusion.

"What do you mean he found her?" the voice continues.

"Fuck... Yes, but it will take time... When?... It'll be difficult... Keep me updated if you know more." Kade. My brain matches the voice with a name like it's a puzzle. Satisfied its work is done, it returns to its fuzzy soft state. The hand continues to run through my hair.

Harsh conversation once again replaces the silence. Around me things bang and feet stomp across the floor. My head lifts and I open my eyes with an effort.

"Relax, I'll be right back. It's okay." Reece's voice works to guide me in the darkness. I smile lazily, letting the floaty feeling engulf me.

Sounds move around me. My brain works to make sense of the sounds and hushed conversations.

———

"ATLAS... HE FOUND HER." SNIPPETS SLIDE THROUGH THE THICK mud in my brain.

"Evacuate..."

"Working on a plan..."

"Two hours."

I want to scream at them to keep it down, but it's not worth the effort.

"She's been through hell... You can't..." Reece growls.

"It is why she came here," Dominick comments calmly.

"Regardless, she needs time."

"Time is a commodity she's out of here. It is one only you can provide now."

My brows knit together. I force thoughts to merge in my brain. Visions form with the words. Edmund's threats come roaring to the forefront. The haze shifts from my mind. Pain sharpens. With an effort I push up and force my eyes to focus.

"Edmund," I whisper. Fear consumes me. His threats against everyone in my life flood through me.

Three sets of eyes pin me to the floor at the whisper of his name.

Dominick is the first to break the silence. "Is there something you've omitted to tell us, Atlas?"

My head falls to my knees. I've put them all in horrible danger.

"Did he find me?" The lack of shock at his name tells me they already knew.

"He did."

"I'm sorry." The words bring shame and a new wave of fear.

Heavy boots thump across the floor. Dominick kneels in front of me. "Atlas, just because it is your name doesn't mean you lift the world alone. You must trust others to help you."

He pushes a hand through his hair.

"We need to get you to safety, and you need to let us know exactly what's going on. No more secrets."

I nod. Words refuse to form.

"Reece," he says as he stands and turns toward the other men. "Get her ready and get her out of here. Kade will give you the details."

"Thank you, Dominick." There is a reverence in his voice.

"Keep her safe."

Two hours later, dressed in a simple pair of jeans and a white T-shirt, I look defiantly at Dominick, my jaw set in a hard line.

"I wasn't asking if you would go. This isn't a request on what you want to do about this situation. I was telling you your next move." His voice reverberates around the room.

The uncharacteristic outburst catches me off-guard.

Outside the office, Ana watches the verbal ping-pong match cautiously. Her eyes flicker up at each heated outburst.

"I can take care of my own problems, Dominick," I demand.

He quirks an eyebrow.

"Sir," I spit. "Coming here was a mistake. I thought..." The words die on my tongue.

"You thought what?" he challenges.

Neither of us backs down. For a long moment, we stand there staring at one another, both refusing to flinch.

Finally, knowing this will only end badly for me, I lower my head.

"If you could have taken care of the situation, it would be over, Atlas. The fact you showed up on my doorstep, so to speak, tells me you are in deeper trouble than you verbalize. It was my hope you would trust me with the extent of it. However, it looks like it is a much bigger situation now."

"You could at least be nice if that's what you think," I counter.

Dominick shakes his head.

"You didn't come for nice. You came for a not so gentle bitch slap of truth, the whip of forgiveness, and direction in the darkness. The path led you here because the weight of your world overwhelms you to near self-destruction and you need a way out. You have an amazing security team and you didn't let them protect you. I don't know what is going on in that head of yours."

Dominick's words hit me hard. I'm not sure why I ended up here. I thought I'd find safety and solace; instead I found harsh words and hard truths. Everything in me knows he's right. Instead of facing this situation, I ran, and now I must continue to run because everyone around me is in danger. Someone I don't even know has paid for my transgression. Guilt pours over me.

"Atlas." Dominick's voice pulls me out of my thoughts. "It's okay to be scared. How we handle the mantle of our decisions and choices determines our character. Let your team get the ground stable again. Spend time with Reece."

"Yes, Sir." The words come unbidden and my head bows. Something in me shifts. It feels like a permanent goodbye, but I don't understand why.

Kade's boots thump across the parquet of the office floor.

"Sir, we have confirmed wheels up in an hour. Terminal 5B. Clearance is granted by the foreign government." Kade states the facts with military precision.

"Thank you, Kade. Is Reece ready to go?"

"He's finalizing personal situations since we're taking them both off-grid."

Dominick nods and looks back at me.

"Safe travels, Atlas." The words are a dismissal.

"Thank you, Sir." I nod and turn to walk out of the room.

CHAPTER ELEVEN

I SLEPT through most of the journey to the island. Even after I awoke, we never spoke. Silence lay like a heavy blanket over us and Reece moved like a man on a mission. Within a few minutes we were driving away from Basseterre, the airport fading in the mirrors.

Reece navigates the roads like driving on the left side of the car on a winding road with potholes and hairpin turns is the most natural thing in the world. The views of the island are breathtaking no matter which direction I look. Fifteen minutes later we pull into a long driveway right above the edge of a cliff. The looming house takes my breath away. Perched on the edge of the cliff, I can see endless vistas of the sea in every direction.

"Come," Reece commands gently.

In front of us lies a modern style house. Its sweeping lines and acres of glass are beguiling in a serene lack of interest to make an impression on its visitors while putting the beauty of the island on full display. He leads us through an eight-foot timber door into a huge foyer. The long infinity pool and Caribbean ocean take center stage through large glass walls for an uninterrupted view. Carefully crafted art complements the stark interior to make it welcoming and inviting. Every room easily flows from one to another.

"Welcome." A man meets us in the foyer. "I will have the luggage delivered to your rooms."

"Thank you, Timothy. I presume everything is in order?" Reece questions as he surveys the house.

"It is, Sir. All the checks are complete and the team installed."

"Excellent."

"Now don't you let that stuffy butler keep ya from my kitchen. I know ya had a long journey," a voice calls from the kitchen to our left, a thick Caribbean accent coating each word.

Reece chuckles.

"Ya might as well bring her in here."

A smile creeps across his face and he nods toward the kitchen.

"Hello, Josephine," Reece says and walks over to kiss the older woman on the cheek.

"Welcome back." She beams.

"Josephine, this is Atlas. Atlas, this is Josephine. She's a personal chef here on the island."

"Ya make it sound like I cater to the whole island." She shakes her head.

"My apologies. She's our family's personal chef. Josephine's been with my family since I was a boy."

"He was a handful, dat one." She gives me a conspiratorial look.

"Don't go talking out of school," Reece replies, smiling at her with affection. "I'm to show Atlas to her room. She's had quite the ordeal recently."

"Shall I send dinner to your room?"

I look at Reece.

"She'll dine with me tonight out on the deck," he confirms.

Josephine nods, grinning in my direction.

Reece's warm hand settles on my back, signaling his desire to leave, and with the lightest pressure, ushers me out of the kitchen. He leads me through the house until we arrive at a large bedroom.

The white walls reach two stories as a gentle breeze blows through it. A sitting area with a chaise lounge takes up half the expansive room with the king-size platform bed occupying the other side. Outside the window, the extravagant calm blue sea sparkles like it's sprinkled with diamond dust as the sunlight glints off the surface. For the first time in weeks, the fear and tension melt away as I stare out at the undulating sea.

CHAPTER TWELVE

"I'VE RUN a bath for you, Ma'am. You'll find everything you need." Timothy breaks the peaceful moment as he walks out of the en suite.

I nod and force a smile. "Thank you."

"If you need anything, please let me know." With an elegant grace, he pivots and walks out of the room.

"I'll leave you to it then," Reece says from behind me. "Dinner will be at six o'clock on the back deck by the pool."

The soft click of the door tells me I am alone.

For a long moment, I stand staring out at the sea. Emotions roll through me like the waves below, moving seamlessly from one end of the spectrum only to return to its start. The weight of the last few months sags across my shoulders and I blow out a harsh breath. I can only hope everything I worked to protect is still standing when this nightmare is over.

Tearing my eyes from the water below, I walk into the luxurious en suite. Steam rises in a light fog off the milky white water in the bath. Sore muscles protest my movements as I undress and give in to its call. Slipping into the bath, the warm water seeps into my pores. Knots in the muscles loosen while each scrape screams out as the Epsom salts pour into the smallest cuts.

I hiss in response to the pain and surrender to the weariness in my body and emotional fatigue. The hot water soothes the tension away until I am almost numb. My head falls back on the thick bath pillow as it cradles my neck, and I once again let my thoughts replay the last few weeks of my life. Edmund's words haunt me. His relentless obsession fills me with uncertainty, and I work to push them away. After the ritual ordeal with Dominick, my entire being feels open, vulnerable, and I chastise myself for the weakness. I lie in the bath until the water cools and then drag myself out of the water.

Standing up, the water sluices from my body in long rivers. I wrap up in the large fluffy towel laid out on a small stand beside the tub. With a flourish, I pull a smaller towel around my hairline and move into the lavish bedroom.

A long maxi dress lies across the bed, and I note the lack of underthings. On the floor sits a pair of soft ballet slippers to match. I look with longing at the thick duvet cover on the bed, wanting nothing more than to dive under it. My body begs to sleep away the exhaustion and find a place to hide from the dark thoughts in my mind. On the bedside table, ship bells ring out, telling me it is already five-thirty.

With care, I dress in the provided outfit and return to the en suite bath to wrap my hair up in a long scarf hanging alongside the other hair accessories. I turn and gaze at my reflection in it. Dark circles line my eyes, bruises bloom across my exposed skin as if to prove my outsides now match my emotional turmoil.

I paste on a smile and turn to meet Reece on the deck.

SOFT BREEZES OF THE OCEAN RIPPLE THE FABRIC OF MY DRESS as I make my way to the sunken lounge area of the deck. In the fire pit, flames dance and pop, moving with unseen music. Reece stares out across the water, the sun just beginning the descent toward the horizon. An explosion of colors mix on the edge to herald the survival of another day.

My feet pad softly across the wooden deck, causing Reece to turn around at my entrance.

"Beautiful," he says. His expression is full of appreciation. The hint of heated lust is right under the surface for only a second before he blinks it away.

"Thank you," I reply and nod.

To my left, Timothy approaches with a silver tray and a glass of wine. I smile softly and take the offering. Without a word, he disappears back into the house.

"Reece." His name is a weight and freedom on my tongue.

He nods. "We'll talk after dinner, Atlas. Everything will be okay. But if Josephine thinks we're letting her hard work go to waste, there'll be hell to pay."

I laugh. It feels odd in my tense frame, but there's something about the last vestige of release which wraps around my frayed emotions, and I let the smile linger on my lips.

"You're beautiful when you smile. Rather, you're always beautiful, but your smile is breathtaking," Reece says, moving toward me as his warm hand lands on my lower back to maneuver us to the dining area.

Neither of us speak through the sumptuous meal. Each course moves in a relaxed pace from one to the next. My wine glass is changed out with each new dish. A delectable vegetable and artichoke pasta course moves easily to a light salad. Once the small salad is complete, Timothy serves the veal scaloppini.

"That was delicious," I comment as the last course is cleared away and the fruit and cheese platter is placed in front of us. For the first time in far too long, I feel calm, pampered, and slightly euphoric.

"Feeling better?" Reece stares at me, one eyebrow quirked upward.

"Yes, thank you."

"It's good to see you relaxing again."

"This place makes it easy to forget many things."

"Yes. There's a serenity about it all. A small island flourishing in the middle of an ocean, far from the huddling masses."

"Or the problems of the world," I mumble.

"We can't just quit the world when there's a slight bump in the road," he challenges.

"A bump? You call this a bump?" I toss back, but my heart isn't ready for a fight.

"Yes I do. You've been looking for this balance for so long, you can't just quit. Together we can fix this problem."

"I'll get it solved. I'm the one Edmund is after. There's no reason for me to put everyone else in danger over it. It's the whole reason I left. To keep everything I love safe." I drain the wine in my glass and stare into its bottom.

"Why did you run, Atlas?"

"You, of all people, are asking me why I ran? Mr. Gabriel, when the scandal hit the front page, you were in my office screaming at me."

"Not my finest hour to be sure."

Under his intense gaze, my world shifts into a different space, but I will not give him the satisfaction to know it.

"Why was my other persona such a problem for you?" I counter to once again find the upper hand.

"You omitted it from our relationship. You didn't trust me," he states.

"Now who's omitting information? I didn't take you for a man without confidence."

Reece chuckles. "I was warned you'd always be a challenge."

For a long minute he simply stares at me, his gaze pinning me in place. When I finally shift under the weight, he smiles.

"When I was younger, I wanted to explore all the forbidden areas of sexuality. I thought being under a Dominatrix would be just the thing. She was abusive and angry. When she discovered my family's wealth, she blackmailed me with pictures I didn't know she'd taken in our sessions. It is the only image of a professional Dominant I'd ever experienced." He pauses, his face twisted in the painful memories. "I struggled to wrap my head around how you could be so submissive with me and yet..."

I shift in my seat until my hand touches his thigh. Electricity curls up my spine at the touch.

"I've always been in control. Everything in my world is under my control. When Dominick taught me how to use it professionally, it was a natural fit. But people aren't one dimensional. Not all needs fit in a box and some just get put away for the greater good," I say with far more conviction than I feel.

Off to our left, Timothy announces that coffee is served in the living room. I break the spell and stand to follow the butler through the house. Behind me, Reece follows close, the heat of his body radiating against my skin.

"I think I will skip coffee and head to bed, if you don't mind. I'm rather tired from today's travel," I say abruptly and continue up the stairs toward the house.

Beside me, Reece catches up and matches my stride. "I will walk you to your room then."

CHAPTER THIRTEEN

I STRETCH. My mind races through the things that need to be done here or there. Shoving the thoughts aside, I roll over, punching the pillow hard in a useless attempt to go back to sleep. My body heaves and sighs at my attempts. Sleep did not come easily during the night. Perfect images of Reece mixed with my ordeal and nightmare until they all blended into a mess I couldn't untangle.

With an effort, I extract myself from the duvet and heave my body out of the bed, then make my way over to the large glass window. My gaze lands on the sea below. It calls to my soul like a balm across the rips and tears. I turn toward the en suite bathroom and lock myself in to get my body back into a presentable shape. For so long, a practiced hand worked over my face and hair to change my appearance and present the necessary mask to the world. Here, I fumble and struggle to understand what it needs to look like when I am done. I sigh at the image in the mirror and pull the bathrobe tight around my form.

When I enter the bedroom, I see Reece, his shoulder propped against the doorframe.

"Good morning, beautiful." He smiles down at me.

I scoff. "I'm far from beautiful."

"Today we're going to the beach. A bit of sun and fun will do you good," he declares. "Below us the cove is private and concealed from a direct approach. No one will know we are there. Above us, the security team will post watch to give us ample time on the off chance I'm wrong. You will enjoy the sea, and getting out a little will be beneficial to you." There's no question in his voice. It is a statement of fact.

"Unfortunately, I didn't pack the necessities for a beach excursion."

"Then it is a good thing the staff is efficient at their job." He nods toward the bed. It is already made without a hint of my tumultuous night. Across it lies a white cover-up and a bikini with matching sandals. He smiles, nods, and turns from his post.

I stare open-mouthed at the garments on the bed. Even prisoners get yard time, I remind myself, and dress in the chosen outfit. A few minutes later, I work my way through the house and out to the terrace.

"Very nice." He picks up the beach equipment under one arm and reaches for my hand with the other. We descend the stone stairs cut into the cliff-side on the other side of the terrace. Thrice I stumble on the way, more interested in the sea than my steps. Each time he reaches out and steadies me before we continue.

Beside a small rock outcropping, a table is laid with breakfast. The smell of coffee wafts through the air and my stomach grumbles in protest. Reece sets down his bundle and hands me a cup of the steaming brew.

I smile my thanks up to him and walk to the water's edge. The quiet, cool surge of the sea swirls around my toes. There is no heavy surge here; it is more seductive and inviting, enticing each step until it swirls above my ankles, then my knees and thighs. The pulsating pull of the water flows around me, its seductive move-ments calling me to swim. It feels like forever since I gave my muscles a good workout. Without knowing the currents and riptides, I stand enjoying the constant ebb and flow across my lower body.

"Are you okay?"

I didn't hear Reece's approach, yet he stands right behind me.

My breath catches in my throat at his light touch and I control my body's reaction.

"Fine." I force a smile.

"The water is cleansing. Each tide wraps around us, draws us in, and washes away our deepest darkness," he whispers in my ear. His hands wrap around my waist, and I lean into him.

"Indeed."

THE IDYLLIC SETTING WORKS ITS MAGIC ON MY BATTERED emotions. Our slow breakfast is filled with relaxed conversation. When we are done, I curl up on the beach blanket. It feels like I can sit and look out at the Caribbean ocean for hours, just breathing in the salty air. My mind is free and thinks about all the places the sea has seen on its journey to this shore. The quiet privacy of the cove is a rare and priceless commodity. My daily life rarely afforded me actual privacy; rather, it was the illusion of it. The tension seeps from my neck and shoulders. Thoughts in my brain unwind.

Reece doesn't hover. Although I note he's alert for anything which might disturb our idyllic setting, there's an air of ease and calm. He's vigilant while being perfectly in the pleasure of the moment. Between us a quiet comfort builds under the mounting tension, while he sits and enjoys the view.

"I'm going for a swim." His voice startles me. "Care to join me?"

"No, thank you." I smile up at him from my content corner of the beach.

He bends down and places a gentle kiss on my forehead.

His toned, sleek body moves as he stretches on the way toward the ocean. For a moment, he wades into the waves. When the water reaches his thigh, he reaches forward and dives as the waves engulf him. It is a good distance until he surfaces, and when he does, his strong shoulders power him through the waves with effortless ease. Reece looks at home in these waters as much as he does on land.

Each stroke pushes him toward the open sea. In mere moments he is at the breakwater. His head vanishes beneath the waves and my stomach drops. He doesn't immediately reappear. Panic surges through my veins. I scramble to my feet and shade my eyes to focus on the distant waters. A hollow feeling settles in my chest when I don't see his form on the horizon at the count of sixty. My body moves unbidden. Steps propel me forward, off the blanket and toward the edge of the water.

My foot comes down on a broken shell. I shift my weight before it slices through the skin but stagger at the force of the shallow wave, losing my balance. The movement causes me to lose my focus on Reece and change to my immediate predicament.

Strong hands steady my waist and I freeze in place. When I don't move, they sweep me behind the knees and pull my body against his chest. He doesn't break stride as he moves back toward the beach.

"I lost my balance," I protest. "It's nothing. I just stepped on something."

"And here I am bringing balance," he quips and continues to move toward the blanket.

Something deep inside turns over in a mix of pain and pleasure. His strong arms wrap around me protectively, dissipating the earlier rise in panic. Above me I admire his handsome face, glistening in the sunlight. Black spikes of lashes accentuate his intense gaze while water runs down the straight of his nose and drips across my skin.

Back on the blanket, he pulls a bottle from the beach bag and offers it while downing the contents of his own. Reece sets the bottle aside and eases closer. His fingers graze the line of my jaw, sending tingles radiating through every nerve ending. My mouth moves to object, but his finger presses against my lips, and he shakes his head.

CHAPTER FOURTEEN

I LOWER my gaze to his mouth. His lips part. He leans toward me but hesitates. Our shallow breaths match in their rhythm. My fingers move up to caress the firm, wet muscles of his chest. They trail down until his racing heartbeat pulses against them.

My eyes never leave his as my fingers work across this chest. Each touch shoots a rush through my body. I lean toward him.

"You're my undoing," he whispers. His hand slides around my waist and pulls me into his chest, and his lips brush against mine.

The salt of the sea mixes with the heat of his body and the undercurrents of power. It is my undoing. Need and desire, long held by my well-built internal walls, floods through me. I open to him without hesitation.

Reece doesn't hesitate. He claims my mouth. We mesh under his commanding kiss. My hands move to his shoulders and continue their upward ascent until they entangle in his hair. I cling to him like his breath gives me life.

His strong arms lower us to the blanket. The heat of the sand underneath the soft fabric cradles our bodies. He continues to plunder the depths of my mouth with soft flicks of his tongue. With the slightest shift, he supports himself on one elbow, as his free hand explores my body.

I work to free my hands to do the same to his.

"Don't move them," he growls against my lips before taking them again.

My hands freeze in place and I give in to the command, letting him control the moment. There is no rush in his movements. The demanding, hard kiss sits in opposition to the soft exploration.

His hand slides down along my hip as if he's trying to memorize every curve and concave on my body. My nipples bead under my suit, begging for his touch, but he continues his skillful journey without haste. Each caress drives me closer to the edge, pushing me in a delirious longing. The world disappears. Only his touch matters.

I gasp and arch when his fingers enclose the apex between my legs. His chuckle vibrates across my skin. Everything in me seeks more of his touch. My breath comes in ragged pants.

"I need you, Atlas," his own irregular breath whispers against my cheek. "I want you."

Hot kisses trail down the side of my face and continue against the curve of my collarbone. My body arches and moves to give more access. His free hand cups my breast while his thumb and forefinger pinch and pull the taut nipple. A shiver races down my spine, and I intwine my legs with his, pushing against his thigh.

"Please." The word drags across my lips.

Everything in me needs to feel him inside. I yearn to feel his body engulfing my own. Here I feel safe and whole. In these moments there are no masks. Under him I am open, vulnerable, and free.

Reece ignores my pleas and pushes my body to the edge. His focus is completely on me, his body taut with restrained power and raw need. I nudge my face against his firm jaw. His head turns, and once again he claims my mouth. The more he gives, the more I need. It isn't enough.

I moan against his mouth. My body pushes against his hand to hasten the orgasm sitting right on the edge.

Cool water splashes against our legs. Above me, Reece shifts away and looks toward the sea. My body screams in protest at the broken connection. With reluctance, he sits up and gazes out to the sea. He rakes his hand through his hair.

I blink as if waking up from a trance.

He turns to me, his mouth tugging into a slow, sardonic grin as he gazes down at the disarray of my swimsuit and my exposed body. With a shake of his head, he reaches down and pulls the suit back into place until I am covered.

The sea continues its determined march toward the blanket. Reece glances back out to sea and releases a sigh.

"It looks like Mother Nature isn't my friend today," he mumbles. "We should get back to the house. High tide will cover this beach in a few minutes. Unless you want to continue. There's always snorkel gear."

My eyebrows shoot toward my hairline, and Reece laughs at my shock.

"What?" He waggles his eyebrows. "It could be fun."

I return his smile, my body thrumming with unspent need.

Without another word, we gather up the remaining supplies and head for the long walk up the stairs back to the house.

ON THE WAY BACK TO THE HOUSE, I FEEL BUOYANT. FOR THE first time in weeks, the weight lifts from my shoulders. Halfway up the cliff, Reece pulls me into a tight embrace.

"Grab the rail. Do not let go," he commands against my ear.

"But the security team can see us."

"You are a professional Dominant. I'm sure your security team sees your performances often."

"That's different," I challenge.

"I know. Draw from the confidence you find there. Do as you're told," he presses.

He grabs my hands, pulling them behind me, and pushes the fingers around the edge of the railing. The warmth of the metal seeps through my skin. His lips touch the tender flesh of my neck and down to my breast. I jerk under his touch, but in an instant his lips move. His hands skim down my stomach and push between my legs.

"Don't let go," he reminds me.

My grip tightens on the rail. With one hand, he frees the strings on my bathing suit top. It falls away effortlessly. His other hand tugs at the strings on my bottoms and seconds later they flutter away.

Never have I felt so blatantly exposed. On the side of a cliff, I stand before Reece naked, with only his command holding me in place. The sea breeze blows across my skin and I shiver.

"Absolutely beautiful." The low growl of his voice heightens my senses and my body races back to the edge.

"Close your eyes," he says as his mouth engulfs my exposed breast.

His hands move up my legs as his mouth moves down to meet them.

"Open. Exposed. Waiting." He breathes against my soaked pussy.

The flash of warmth makes my breath catch. When he moves back up my body, I twist in frustration. He weaves a path of kisses over my hip and up my stomach until he engulfs the other breast.

"Please," I beg, everything in me crying out its need for him.

"Please what?" His hot breath hovers over my nipple and I arch into him.

"Kiss me. Lick me. Fuck me." My pleas rush out without thought. My body burns with a need I've never let myself feel.

His hot mouth licks and sucks the hard bud. My hands grip the rail harder. His teeth graze the tender skin and clamp down. The sharp pain mixes with the mounting pleasure and I push into it. He soothes the ache with a gentle lap of his tongue. With a slight shift, he repeats the process on the other nipple.

The sound of his mouth moving over my nipples mixes with the distant sound of the sea and I am lost under his touch.

"More," I beg openly. Everything in me craves his touch and his command. Here there is freedom from the weight of the world. A wave of peace crashes over me.

In response, a finger trails through my soaked pussy, a slow caress from the bottom through the top. The intimate touch threatens to shatter me, but he stops right on the edge. His finger continues to move in a slow rhythm.

"Or maybe this is what you'd like instead."

The tip of his tongue repeats the same path. My hips shoot forward.

"That. Please!" I moan.

My body shivers in response. His tongue flicks the edge of my clit before plummeting inside, only to repeat the process. Under me, my legs quiver with effort.

When I think I can take just one more touch before exploding, his mouth moves away. My body screams, and my eyes fly open.

A smirk plays at the edge of his lips.

My mind is a jumble of thoughts, and my body refuses to move from the spot.

Reece steps away and retrieves my cover-up from the beach bag. He turns and faces me, his fingers cupping my chin and tilting my head back.

"You are good at dealing with pain. It helps you build walls against the world and creates a physical way to let it all out. But what no one realizes"—he pauses and pulls back to watch my face—"is you're completely defenseless when it comes to overwhelming plea-sure. When what you really need is to dangle on the edge of pleasure, craving it to mesh with the pain until you find the explosion in the freedom under someone else's command. If only for a moment to rest."

A sudden chill runs across my skin from the loss of warmth from the nearness of his body. I shiver as goosebumps run frantically up my arms.

"Let's go shower."

He brushes a gentle kiss against my forehead and turns to move up the remaining stairs. I stare after him, my body screaming with need and my mind racing at his words.

I WORK MY WAY UP THE STEEP STAIRS. EACH STEP MAKES MY legs burn. It's been weeks since I've seen the inside of a gym, and I'm paying for it. The long climb helps me find center. My nerves still buzz from his touch, and I smile. It is the first real smile to touch my lips since I walked away from everyone and everything. I let the lightness melt over me as I round the last flight. At the top, Reece smiles down at me.

"Sir. You have a call on the Sat phone," Timothy announces behind him.

"Tell them I'm on my way," he calls out to acknowledge the information. His eyes never leave mine.

I climb the final step. His strong arms engulf me while his lips graze mine.

"Looks like I need to take care of some business. Go take a shower and get dressed. We'll curl up and watch the sunset over dinner."

My smile dips in disappointment when I realize I will shower alone but returns at the thought of his arms around me as we watch another day end together.

"And Atlas—" he starts.

"Yes, Sir." The words roll off my tongue.

"Don't come or the pain will contain no pleasure." He whispers the words across my skin.

I shiver in response. My mind screams at his insolence to think he could issue such a command. Ripples of need rip through my body, once again igniting the smoldering inferno. It is my heart which responds to the quiet space he offers in the chaos and understanding of my darkest needs.

"As you wish, Sir." A mischievous smile is the only tell of the internal war as I walk past him.

His hand slaps across my ass as I pass, and I wiggle it in answer but continue to move toward the house. I barely notice anyone as I make my way to the en suite shower.

With a flick of my wrist, the shower responds. The water is instantly warm. With a quick step out of my cover-up, I step under the water.

I brace my feet wide apart and rest my hands against the wall. The hot water runs in rivulets down my body from above while the jets work against my shoulders and lower back, trickling down my ass and dripping off my hard nipples. Need spikes through me and his words ring through my mind. An image of his taut, hard body next to mine springs forward unbidden, and I let out a groan.

I pick up the loofah and work it over across my skin in an attempt to numb the need calling for his touch, trying to focus on anything but the image of his body against mine. Here, alone, I can let my guard down, imagining what it would be like to let him in and feel his protection engulf me. I fantasize about what it would be like to have someone able to help lift my world. I allow myself to take it to the brightest and darkest recess of my emotions and mind. Further than I've ever allowed myself to believe is possible.

My finger brushes against my soaked pussy and I groan. I need a release. My mind wars with my heart over the decision. In resignation, my hand drops away, and my body quivers at its absence.

The water washes away my last vestiges of control. With an effort, I turn off the shower and wrap the large towel around my body. I let my mind drift as I dress in the bright teal-colored maxi dress laying on the bed.

My mind wanders to what could be keeping Reece when Timothy arrives with a tray of cucumber mint water and fresh fruit.

"I thought you might like a light refreshment after your time in the sun." He sets the tray on the side table and walks out of the room.

I pick up a glass of water and let its soothing combination work through me. Restless, I pick up the remote beside the tray and flip on the seventy-inch television in the seating area. Flipping through the satellite guide, I choose a Washington DC station. The commercial drones on about the world's best towel. I smile at the return of some normalcy in my world.

CHAPTER FIFTEEN

"THIS IS Jon Dause at the EPN Center with breaking news. The Empyrean Club in Washington DC, a well-known sex club, has been evacuated because of a threat posted on the front door of the club. DC's Metro Police Department is on the scene investigating now. EPN's Janet Smith joins me now, on location outside the club gates. Janet, what's happening there right now?"

My head spins toward the television as a picture of the club comes into view from a helicopter's angle. Police tape wraps its way around the expansive front and semi-circular driveway. Outside the gates, a large crowd gathers and intermingles with the crush of news vans.

"John, I'm standing outside the gates of the infamous Empyrean Club. We've been here since close to nine o'clock Eastern Time this morning, and from what we understand, a threat was posted on the club's front door."

I step toward the television. My mind erupts in fear, anger, and helplessness as I watch the images play across the large screen.

"Details remain sketchy, but an anonymous tip came into our

studio shortly after the police arrived on scene. The following short clip gives us the only details of the situation."

A large blood-covered knife sticks out of the enormous front door. A thousand memories flood my brain. Under the knife, a piece of paper flutters in the breeze. The camera blurs on the paper in an attempt to focus. When it comes into view, the paper blows against the door. The words work to penetrate the defenses in my mind.

"If I can't have you, then I will destroy you."

A scream rips from my throat.

The glass in my hand shatters against the floor as my body shakes uncontrollably.

Splinters of glass create shimmering puddles of fragments around my bare feet as I stare at the television.

"No matter your feelings about the club, this threat is horrifying," the newscaster continues but is drowned out by the rumble of footfalls that fill the house. I turn toward the first person through the door. A satellite phone is next to Reece's ear as his head swivels between me and the images flashing across the television screen.

My knees buckle. The phone flies across the room. Strong arms engulf me as they sweep behind my knees before I make it to the floor.

"Turn that damn television off!" he roars to the next body entering the room as he sets me on the bed.

Tears stream in rivers down my face. A weight sits heavy in my chest. Panic claws up my throat. Reece pulls me into his lap and picks up the phone. His hand smooths across my hair.

"Yes. Someone in this house failed to disconnect the television in her room," he growls into the phone. The rumble in his chest is loud against my ear. "Samantha?... Good. Call Ian and Jillian; they may be able to give some insight... Yes... I know."

Sobs wrack my body but sound refuses release. The world around me spins as it erupts in chaos. Reece's hand never leaves me.

"Dominick?" The question hangs in the air. "Then FIND him!

This is your wheelhouse, Kade. It's time we find this bastard and clean up this mess... Keep me informed."

Reece mumbles a curse under his breath and pulls me up against his chest.

"It will be okay," he murmurs against my hair.

I shake my head. His words clash against the obvious reality. I want to scream that it will never be okay. Everything in me wants to throw things and rage at the universe, but my body refuses my demands.

"This will sting, Atlas, but it's for the best." He clamps down on my arm. The strong smell of alcohol wafts through the air right before the needle slams home in my arm. I try to pull away, but his grip is too strong and the effects of the drug are immediate.

All my muscles slacken. Darkness creeps on the edge of my vision.

"Don't. This isn't fair." I mumble the words.

"It has nothing to do with fair, Atlas. I protect what is mine." The darkness swallows his words as my world fades away.

CHAPTER SIXTEEN

OUTSIDE MY WINDOW the weather refuses to cooperate. The sea undulates calmly against my every demand for a storm to swell and release my agony.

Instead, the brightest of days casts few shadows from a cloudless sky. Without thought, I raise the glass to my lips. The dark liquid pours across them, engulfing my tongue with a bittersweet finish as it runs in a stream down my throat. It does little for the mood or my rising temper, only adding to the melancholy consuming me in ways I no longer try to explain to myself or anyone else. All attempts for those around me to reach me fail because I want them to.

Across the room, the hard click of leather soles on the hardwood floors alerts me to his presence. Even then I do not raise my head; instead I push further inside and take another long drink. His masculine smell surrounds me. Everything in me screams to let down my guard, but I only raise it higher in personal defiance, knowing he owns the keys to my soul if he uses them. If he can find the lock to the walls.

His fingers caress a light trail down my face. For a moment I let my eyes shut, the movement carrying me away from the darkness.

Memories of a softer time when I wanted to give in to his demands, a time when the world didn't create the constant lashing of my soul. His thumb reaches my chin, and I pull from his grasp.

"How many days since you found out about the club?" His soft tone pushes the words toward me as if to gauge my reaction.

"Fifteen." I spit the words from my mouth. "Fifteen days since the world found out that I'm an idiot."

"How do you know the count?"

I debate the answer. Silence hangs in the air, but neither of us move to soften the tension.

With a deep sigh, I finally relent. "Because I mark each one on a makeshift calendar." I shrug to prove it doesn't bother me. "The days all run into one another like an oozing mass with no separation otherwise."

"Don't you think it is been enough time?"

"Define enough. Enough time that you want to walk out the door because it's no longer easy? Enough because I should suddenly put all this behind me? Enough because the world has gone stark raving mad without me? Enough because..." Anger pours from me, but the emotion isn't the reason I stare out the window. It is another tactic to push him away. With this latest threat, it is obvious anyone close to me is in danger, and I will not have any more blood on my hands.

"The definition of enough, when I originally walked in here, was the impatient cessation of a non-desired set of behaviors, thoughts and speech patterns. However, it is now more of a change to the question—do you believe you've gone down this path to the point in which you wish to change the direction for a more productive one?"

I sit stock still. Nothing in me, outside the shallow rise and fall of my chest, moves in any meaningful way. His words hit a nerve. I want to scream, but all of my emotions short circuit.

"I have no idea how to do it. I'm lost." The words pass my lips without thought. As soon as I hear them around us, I want to take them back.

His fingers cup my chin and pull my face around until my only choices are to look at him or close my eyes away from him. From the edge of my eye, a tear escapes. I want to banish it with the full brunt of my anger and the back of my hand, but the look in his eye holds me captive.

"You aren't lost, my dear."

"Then I am weak. An intolerable condition to be sure." My words whip back at him.

A soft chuckle rises from his chest, and he closes his eyes and shakes his head. When he settles again, his piercing stare holds me hard in place. "There is nothing weak about you."

"Look at me!" I know I look a mess. "The thoughts in my head run like hamsters on a wheel, and my social skills are nonexistent."

"I am. Amid everything, you are the strongest, most beautiful woman I know."

I try to shake my head, but his fingers tighten their grasp. "Flattery will get you nowhere."

"It's not flattery, I assure you. When is the last time you exercised?"

The out-of-place question causes my eyebrows to furl in both thought and realization. "I... I... I don't know."

"I see." His fingers let go of my chin. "We are still in a power-based dynamic?"

"I presume so." The reality of the question dawns across the deep, thick mud entrapping my mind.

"As such, you and I are bound by a contractual arrangement. Under said agreement, you are to maintain a fitness regimen and to take care of your body, mind and emotions."

"Have you paid attention to the recent destruction of my life?"

"I witnessed, and fell victim, to some very large missteps of yours. These are true statements. Yet here we are."

"Yes. Here we are. Unless you want out, which I would perfectly understand."

"Do you wish to abide by your contract or end the relationship?

One is an easier road than the other, though it may not be the one you think."

The turn of my statement back on me abrades my raw emotions. Nothing in me is ready for this question. Simplistic, as if it were a wardrobe decision rather than one which could alter both our lives.

"It's time to be strong or to wallow in the darkness which surrounds you, Atlas. What say you?"

CHAPTER SEVENTEEN

I CLOSE my eyes and try to take a deep, cleansing breath to stave off the panic. Sharp stabs of dread and fear grab my chest, and the simple act of inhaling takes more strength than necessary.

"You're safe, Atlas. I'm here."

With an effort, I crack one eye open and stare into his eyes. There is a mixture of concern and hope. The unexpected softness holds me captive, and I do my best to focus on him.

"I'm fine." The words pass across my lips in an odd mixture of relief and defense. It is my standard reply. It signals my lack of desire to discuss uncomfortable internal issues. No matter how bad things are, they are always fine.

His eyes narrow at my flippant response. Displeasure clouds his features.

"Feeling Insecure, Neurotic, and Emotional. I'd agree with that answer."

My body shakes under his stare. The self-reliant, independent woman inside screams she doesn't need him or anyone else, but the vulnerable part wants nothing more than to run to him for protection. A thousand feelings rage through me. I feel caught. He knows I'm fighting back a wave of rising panic. For weeks I've battled the attacks alone.

"Breathe through it." His voice is soft.

With an effort, I work to catch my breath. When I find a semblance of center, I take another sip of wine.

"How often do those occur?"

"I don't keep track." I stare into my glass, refusing to meet his eyes.

From the corner of my eye I see him nod slightly.

"I've lost my place in your world. In your darkest moment, I did not provide you what you needed. I have to earn your trust and my place back. To do it, I have to start with your mind. Lead you out of this oppressive darkness. Show you I can keep you safe. I can only apologize for failing you. I thought you needed space to deal with all the things in your world. Sorry will never be enough for allowing you to believe I abandoned you. I've been right here all along."

I let out a breath in a deep sigh. His words bite to my core. Without thought, my shoulders curl forward to protect me from an invisible harm imagined in my mind.

"I'm sorry you feel alone amid this raging storm in your life."

His words bring a cacophony of emotions. They tumble through me. Trepidation, regret, sorrow, anticipation, hope, and fear—all weave through his words.

With a shrug, I continue to stare into my glass. "It's fine."

Beside me his body tenses. "Eyes on me."

In reaction to his words, my eyes lift and stare into his.

"Until we dissolve this relationship, I demand complete honesty. Your lack of openness helped pave the way to this point. From here on, it will be the most important rule between us. I will require you to meet this without question. That which yields is not always weak, neither does failure prove weakness. It is when we do not make the necessary adjustments that causes the problem. If you think you can meet this requirement going forward, then reply with a more honest answer."

The unexpected response charges straight through me. Like a life ring thrown into the stormy sea, I allow his words to wash over me. For a moment, the emotional guard I've so long held drops and hope seeps into the darkness. I am scared, needy and wounded. All I long to do is to find peace even if it is at his feet. A place where I felt safe, no matter what he demanded.

With an effort, the words whisper out. "I can accept your terms."

"Own the words. Say them with confidence and conviction. You are a strong woman and words are far too easily wasted."

Anger flashes through me and on its heels, a wave of relief. Maybe he could hold up my world, if only for a moment. With more confidence, I push the words forward again.

"I can accept your terms, Sir."

"Much better. There's hope you will return to me yet, rather than this colorless being who sit before me."

I glare at him.

"There is still fire in you. Good. You have no business kneeling at my feet or standing at my side if you aren't strong enough to know your own mind. You know this."

I TREMBLE UNDER THE WEIGHT OF HIS WORDS, LETTING A LONG silence linger between us.

"It's not fine, Reece." The words come out in a painful rush. "When our world blew apart, you added to it. I didn't make the scandal, but I also didn't get the chance to tell you how it hurt me too. You emotionally left me when I needed you the most. Stormed into my office and laid everything at my feet. When everything became hard, you walked away."

For a long time he holds my gaze. "As did you."

The smack of his words rushes through me. I think of Kade and Samantha dealing with the club and try to push down the helpless feeling.

"I admit, when Kade called from Dominick's, I hesitated," Reece said. "You are so strong, I believed my help would be a hinderance. From all appearances, you had it all together until you didn't. Then you were gone. You didn't let anyone into what was happening."

"My name means a lifter of worlds, yet I failed."

"Not even the mythical god could do it alone. You two have something in common; you both needed help. He tried to trick others to do it for him. Your pride makes you fall because you refuse to allow others to help."

He lets the words hang in the silence.

"From now on, we are removing words from your vocabulary which do not allow us to be open. Starting with the word fine. Am I clear?"

With a slow nod, I agree.

"The best way for us to move forward is to take a step backwards. If you agree to remain in the terms of our relationship, we will begin again."

"We can't go back to... "

"Stop. It wasn't a point of negotiation. There are enough issues on the table without inviting more problems to the party. Do you agree to my terms?"

"Yes." A mass of conflicting emotions rushes through me.

"Do you agree to taking a step back and working from the beginning?"

I pause. His expression doesn't change as he waits for my reply.

"How can I...." I start.

"It was a yes or no question." His voice is firm.

With a sigh, I let my eyes close in defiance of my own thoughts. "Yes."

A smile creeps across his face.

"Thank you for putting your trust in me. I hold the responsibility in the highest regard. You are mine and I will not fail again. We will not fail again."

I want to believe him. Everything in me wants to follow. If I hadn't pushed him away. My brow furrows at the thought.

"What thoughts are going through your mind?"

Without consideration of the words, I open my mouth to say 'Nothing.' When my eyes meet his, I freeze before the word can be expressed.

"I am tired. I know there is much to discuss. I do not know if I will disappoint you as I have so recently. I do not want to fail."

"Atlas, there is much to discuss, but it would not be productive with you in this state. You are never a disappointment, and we all stumble. Let's have dinner and make plans to discuss the way forward tomorrow afternoon."

CHAPTER EIGHTEEN

FOR MONTHS I've dealt with insomnia, but there is something different this time. No amount of white noise or calming words can break me out of the need to twist and turn in the bed. I pace in front of the window, staring out into the dark, the white caps of the waves shimmering in the spotlights.

His words consumed my entire night. Any version of training makes nervousness race through me. I've been in the lifestyle for so long it should be second nature. Yet I find myself as giddy as a newbie about starting over while afraid of losing everything. Logic moves against emotions, and I sigh.

I grab my robe and walk down the hall to the kitchen. With practiced movements, I put the kettle on the stove. Thoughts spin as I try to make sense of why he wants the relationship to 'restart' as if I'm new. A time where the dance is about the structure needed to form respect. I wonder if I can open enough to trust. I wonder if he'll be there to catch me when I fall.

The kettle whistles. I pour near boiling water over the Earl Grey teabag. There was a time when I loved the simple ritual of loose tea, but even that simple pleasure has escaped from my world.

The gray skies threaten my mood. With a shake of my head, I force the path of my thoughts to stop. Reece isn't putting this path in front of me because I am inadequate; he's doing it so I can find peace. When I look at it through a dominant lens, the one I use in most of my life, it makes far more sense. In many ways it is exactly how I would handle this situation. But when I let the buried parts stretch their legs and roam free, I find my emotions tenuous.

The crushing issues seep in and I feel alone.

I take a long sip of tea.

What will it be like to hand over the mantle of dominance? Is it even possible? Dominick formed me until my perspective was shaped to see the world in terms of power and control. A place where you either give or receive. The clear definition is more necessary in a business. What will it be like to force a change? Will he lead in a way which helps lift my world or will he find the task too onerous, leaving me under the crushing weight as it lands against my shoulders once more?

"I'm too old for this nonsense." My voice echoes off the kitchen walls.

"You are far from old." Reece's voice answers my statement. His tall frame steps out of the shadows. My eyes roam his bare chest, causing my breath to catch.

"Atlas." He walks to me, brushing a light kiss across my forehead. "You are up early."

"I couldn't sleep."

"What's wrong?" Concern laces his tone.

"Nothing. Things are fin... " The words die on my lips. My eyes drop and I gaze into the mug.

From the edge of my view, I see his eyebrows lift slightly. "Would you like to try that again?"

I exhale but don't immediately speak.

Beside me, his body tenses, but he doesn't move.

"I did not sleep. Thoughts ran through my head in dark intervals. I'm being hunted by a madman who was my client. We spent hours in private sessions together. Now there's a bloody knife with a note threatening to destroy me on the front door of my club. I haven't seen home in months and I wonder how it came to this point."

"A much better start. The situation with your former client is in the hands of the authorities. There is nothing you can do about it."

The air sits heavy with unspoken words.

"And? Is that all that kept you from slumber?" His firm touch rubs circles across my tense shoulder.

"I'm concerned about our conversation yesterday." My eyes do not lift.

"Why?"

"It threatens my view. I'm a Dominant. It is my job to wield power and control situations for the betterment of those around me. You... you touch a different piece."

"Do you think a submissive is weaker or less than a dominant?" he challenges. "Are those who kneel before you not your equal?"

A smile plays on the edge of his lips. I know he's playing with me, but I rise to the challenge anyway.

"You can't have a power exchange of unequals." My head jerks up and I stare at him.

"Of course you can't, but you can have a relationship which is misinterpreted as such. A person without personal power can't give away what they do not own. They may cower in fear, tremble under the abusive weight of a bully or succumb to abuse; however, that is not a power exchange and you know it."

I nod.

"Now. Tell me again why a Dominant cannot take solace as a submissive to an equal?"

"It proves they are incapable of being a Dominant." My fear pours out without hesitation. "They bow because they can't control their own world. It is..."

I don't finish the sentence because even I don't believe it is true.

"You are far harder of a judge on yourself than need be. A human trait but one which is less desirable for us moving forward."

"I know my own faults and weakness," I acknowledge.

"No, you dwell on them. Submission is many things. Full of what all the parties bring to the dance. There is no right or wrong way to do any of this. You know this. You teach it."

"Yes. I'm so overwhelmed I no longer know where to grab to find stability."

"This is why you desire to submit. A place to lay down the world and let someone who is capable and willing lift it while you rest."

"I've never thought of it that way before," I acknowledge.

His hands continue to caress my back. The muscles in my shoulder loosen, and I mull over his words.

"Look at all the things we would miss if you simply replied with 'fine' to my earlier question," he whispers against my ear. "Now go get your bathing suit on, it's time for laps in the pool. You're thinking too much and it's too early to put across my lap to make it stop. So I'll put you in my lap pool instead."

I pull from his grasp and spin around.

His easy smile catches me off-guard.

I nod.

His words ignite something in me I've not felt in far too long.

CHAPTER NINETEEN

"GOOD MORNING, YOU TWO," Josephine calls from the edge of the kitchen.

We turn and smile at her in unison.

"Get out of my kitchen. I need to cook the Master of the house his breakfast or there will be trouble." She winks at Reece.

He chuckles.

"Something I wish more people around here would understand." He throws me a look.

I roll my eyes and shake my head.

"Go get dressed, Atlas. I'll meet you poolside in ten minutes."

"Yes, Sir." The words flow without thought.

Josephine starts to make a comment, but a look from Reece stops her before a sound ekes out of her mouth.

I laugh to myself. It is a look I've thrown many times with the same result but one which I've rarely received. With a soft pivot, I pad back to my room to dress.

On the horizon, the first rays of the sun sneak over the horizon through the patches of broken clouds. The storm abates just as my mood lifts. With a smile, I change into a one-piece bathing suit, tentatively stretching my body, pulling tight muscles taut and then releasing them.

Ten minutes later, I walk onto the terrace. Reece stands behind the pool staring out over the sea. The steam from his mug rises, kissing his skin, and I find myself jealous of it. I scoff at the strange thought.

Reece turns around at the sound and smiles.

"Have you stretched?"

"Yes," I state and look at the glassy water of the pool.

"Then in the water you go." His hand moves in a flourish toward the pool, and he bows.

"Thank you, kind Sir," I say and roll my eyes, tossing the towel on the nearest chair.

I hit the water in a fast, shallow dive and come up halfway across the long lap pool. The cool water wakes up every sense. On the surface, I stroke to the end of the lane and flip to turn around and swim back. When I touch the other side I am winded, and the effects of the short swim burn through my muscles.

"Another one," Reece says from the pool deck.

I glare at him and he only smiles. With a strong kick, I glide under the water and once again surface halfway down the lane. My strokes are slower. Each breath is an effort. I chastise myself for not working out as I make the turn back toward Reece.

When I tag the wall, I hear him command, "Another one" above me, and the whole cycle starts again. For the next half hour, he pushes me. Every time I touch the wall, his command is simple and sends me back down the pool for another lap.

Muscles scream with each stroke. My lungs burn. I touch the wall and hear the familiar command. This time, I flip on my back and stroke backwards. Above me I see him smile and nod.

After two more laps, my body struggles in the water. When my fingers graze against the wall, I grasp the edge. Every breath is a gasp.

"Let's get some breakfast," Reece says and walks away from the poolside.

I stare after him. My body hangs limp in the water as I stare out to sea. The sunrise is an explosion of color, and I watch it until my breath returns to normal. Pushing off the wall, I glide to the pool ladder and climb out. Water sluices from my body. The change makes it heavier as I walk to my towel.

When I arrive at the table, Reece looks up from his tablet.

"How are you feeling, Atlas?"

"Tired."

"Looks like we need to do this every day then." He smirks.

"Sadist."

"A well-known fact. You'll find I don't just use the conventional toys and activities."

"Noted."

"Good. Now eat some breakfast. The day is just getting started."

"IN YOUR PERFECT WORLD, HOW DEEP DOWN THE RABBIT HOLE would you go?" Reece asks casually.

My movement stops mid-bite and I work to swallow the food in my mouth. I reach for a glass of water to aid my distress. The cool liquid coats my mouth and gives me time to form an answer.

"I don't understand your question," I reply to stall for more time. Without a doubt I know exactly what he's asking me. He wants to know if I want to know where this all fits in my world. It breaks my temporary illusion of peace. My mind races and screams not to answer the question.

"Stop stalling." The words are not harsh but direct.

For a long minute we watch each other.

"I'm curious to know how deep I can go without losing a step in the other parts of my world."

Reece nods and stabs the vegetable omelet with his fork.

"I saw an openness and vulnerability about you at Dominick's."

Memories of my 'redemption' pour through me. It is a need I rarely address.

"Yes," I confirm. "He made me."

"Your creator, as he put it." His casual tone is at odd with the conversation.

"How can I give you what you need?"

"Understand me." He quirks an eyebrow.

"Isn't that what every Dominant says to a submissive?" I mock him. "'How can I understand you and fulfill your needs?' Come on, Reece, you're better than this."

"Hark, is that a hint of Alexandra I hear?" he teases.

"Maybe. I've been feeling less like Alexandra and more like Atlas fallen." I force a smile.

"That's what we're here to fix."

"You need to learn all of me. When this 'little vacation' is over, the world will slam right back down on my shoulders and the mess it's in will be my responsibility."

"Our responsibility," he corrects. "You are so many things. The duplicity of your life is astounding, but it leaves you empty in so many places."

"Then fill those places." It is a simple but weighty statement.

"Are you willing to put in the work to make it happen?"

"Are you?" The words grace my lips in a full challenge.

I hold my breath. The hope of being understood hangs in the air.

"I am," he states and looks into my eyes. Something new lights behind them.

"Then so am I." I push back with the same force.

"See how easy it can be when you agree with me, pet?" An enigmatic smile snakes across his face, transforming into a mischievous grin.

The term of endearment runs a warm tingle across my skin. Realization dawns. This is new. Safe. Here we sit, sparring, talking about every aspect of me in a single conversation, and I feel safe. It is both disarming and exciting.

"Something's changed," I parry.

"More like something is released. You aren't a singular facet. No one set of anything serves all of your needs. When I said I'd failed you, it wasn't in need or want. You seemed perfectly put together. When we were together, you submitted so easily. Every motion, every position, every command carried out. I never imagined it was the smallest part of you. My failing is putting a label on you, only letting my experience with others dictate my reactions and inter-actions."

"Your move, Sir." I smile.

He smiles at me and cups my chin.

"How far down the rabbit hole do you want to go?"

"I already live in this land, Mr. Gabriel. Bring it."

He releases my chin, his whole body shaking in laughter.

"Oh, my dear Atlas, I plan to bring it to all your masks."

"We welcome it."

Silence falls across the table. Reece picks up his fork and continues his breakfast. I follow his lead as we continue the meal in amenable silence.

With each bite, I replay the conversation in my head. Processing it, opening to it, and letting hope bloom from it.

Reece finishes his breakfast and breaks the silence. "I want us to go as deep as we can go together. To delight in your accomplish-ments, watch you artfully work your duplicity, and see you enjoy setting it all down at my feet when you need to rest."

With a deep breath, I smile. "I'd like that too."

"Good. While we can't erase our history, nor would I want to," he says with a knowing look. "I believe we can reset it. To that end, let me start."

With that, he reaches his hand over the table in a gesture to shake mine. When I lift mine to his, he pumps it a couple of times. "Hi, I'm Reece and I will be your Dominant and partner on this journey."

A boyish grin blooms across his face, and I can't help but laugh. For the first time in months something in my chest loosens.

I laugh out loud at the pure ridiculousness of the whole scene.

"Now there's a sound I'll delight in hearing often—along with other sounds, to be sure. I want all of you, no matter what name."

A genuine smile etches across my face as I look up at him.

"Not everything has to be hard in a dynamic relationship, you know. Sometimes things are hard or stoic, and sometimes they are soft and funny." His fingers graze my chin.

"An excellent observation."

"I'm glad you agree. Since you're a writer, and I hear you were writing a book, I thought you could spend the rest of the day writing."

I groan, thinking about the book Samantha had been pushing me to finish when I walked away.

"I want you to write about you. You'll find everything you need in your room. Because of our current circumstances, everything is air-gapped with few exceptions. I'm sure you'll understand."

"As you say, Sir." Sarcasm drips on the edge of my tone and I chuckle.

Reece smiles knowingly.

"I think I'll take a shower," I say as I slide from my chair.

"Want some company?" Reece asks but doesn't move.

"I thought you'd never ask." My voice is tight and a thrill of anticipation runs through me.

CHAPTER TWENTY

MY STEPS ARE LIGHTER as I move back to my bedroom and walk straight to the shower. With a flick of my wrist, the water pours from the rain showerhead. Muscles quiver from their earlier exertion as I undress. The bathing suit hits the floor.

"Beautiful," Reece mumbles from the door.

I spin around to face him.

"I thought you might not be coming."

The space fills with steam and the mirror clouds, blocking our reflection.

"Had to attend to a couple of things." The words hang in the air without further explanation.

"You've got too many clothes on, Mr. Gabriel," I say and turn to step into the shower.

The warm water runs against my tight muscles. Behind me, I hear Reece step into the shower.

"Was that an edge of impertinence I heard?" he asks against my ear.

"Oh, whatever could you mean?" The deep Southern accent is foreign on my tongue, but it makes me smile.

"So this is how you're going to play it."

His fingers snake through my hair. My breath stutters. His fist tightens, and I moan. With one smooth motion, he spins me around until I face him, his hand still tangled in my hair. The ferocity of heat in his eyes matches my own. My head pulls back, forcing my lips to part. Then his mouth is on mine. Commanding, probing, and controlling. Each movement demands I open to him.

Reece releases his grip.

"Turn around and place your hands on the shower wall." His voice is gravelly.

I pause and look at him.

"When I give you an order, I expect it to be followed immediately and without question."

He slaps the side of my thigh. The wet skin increases the pain, and I cry out.

"When I give you an order, I expect it to be followed," he growls. My heart flutters. I'm caught between wanting to challenge him and giving in to the shift I feel under his piercing stare.

"Now, Atlas."

His firm command turns my core molten. I turn around, staring at the marble tile, and place my hands on it.

Behind me I hear him move. His touch is slick with shower gel. There's nothing rushed in his movements. Each one explores every curve and hollow of my body, igniting my skin.

"Spread your legs." He doesn't wait for me to decide, nudging them apart with his foot.

His hand clamps down over my pussy. My ass pushes back into his groin, and I groan. The mix of pain and pleasure shoots through me. The faint tear of foil settles around me and I look back. A sharp smack rings out against my ass.

"Eyes front."

"Yes, Sir." The last vestige of my defenses fall. My traitorous body begs him to take what he needs.

He wraps an arm around my waist and fists my hair with the other. His cock nudges the edge of my entrance.

"I won't be gentle."

"Prove it." The last of my challenge pushes across my lips.

I NEED TO KNOW HE CAN TAKE AS GOOD AS HE GIVES. THAT NO matter how much he loves me, the edge won't dull. Not only can he keep me safe from the world, he can push me through the deepest darkness.

His cock breaches the edge of my entrance. My muscles spasm and my hands drop from the wall.

"Please," I beg him. I need to feel his control.

"Hands on the wall," he snaps.

My hands fly back into position.

He growls behind me and shoves in hard. I gasp at the sudden pain and pleasure. Behind me, Reece freezes in place, buried deep, his arm around my waist.

I catch my breath as he eases out of me. Then plows back in again.

Exquisite pleasure mixes with the pain of my muscles and I moan. There is nothing gentle about the way he moves. Each stroke pounds into me.

Fingers splay against the cool tile. My arms shake in an effort to hold me up. The fatigued muscles scream out, but I ignore them and focus only on the relentless pounding. I arch and open, silently begging for more. Everything else melts away.

Here I am his. There's nothing more I need to do other than obey. Here the world lifts off my shoulders and there's only one focus. I drown in the sensation, his hard cock demanding more from my body.

My muscles clamp down.

"Don't you dare come," he growls against my ear.

Weeks of tension sit right on the edge. My body demands release. I hold the edge as long as I can until it slips through my grasp. Tight muscles clamp down on his cock and I hear him groan. A low moan erupts from somewhere in the depths of my soul as the orgasm crashes across me.

He reaches around and slaps my clit hard. The pain pushes me back across the abyss as the waves of pleasure take me across it.

Reece grips my hips hard and slams into me.

"Next time, you will ask permission," he says through clenched teeth. It makes me happy that I'm not the only one struggling. I hear him curse softly before impaling me. The warmth of his orgasm pulls into me through the condom. Aftershocks race through my body. My leg muscles fail, and I start to collapse.

His strong arms catch me, pulling my body into his. Sharp pain radiates through my shoulder as he bites hard into it. I cry out.

"Maybe next time you'll remember your place."

The water runs down our intertwined bodies as we pant to catch our breaths.

"I'm sorry."

"For what?"

"Not asking."

I feel lips smile across my shoulder.

"I'm not."

He places kisses down my back, then returns to the apex of my spine and nips it.

Tears spring to my eyes. My body trembles.

Reece eases out of me as his arm wraps around me and helps me out of the shower. He engulfs me in a giant bath sheet and pulls the ends together. I sob in a shuddered release. He sweeps me into his arms and steps out of the shower.

"I told you pleasure was your undoing. Welcome home, pet."

Wordlessly, I lay my head on his shoulder. The world is calm. Hope springs forward in the void. In this place I believe I can be all the things my world demands as long as he's there with me.

CHAPTER TWENTY-ONE

I AWAKE with a start and sit upright in bed. My mind lingers in a fuzzy, thick fog. Across the room, Reece's eyes linger on me, his tablet lit up in his lap.

"Welcome back, pet." He smiles. "If you keep looking at me like that, I'll come over there and show you what round two feels like."

"Promises, promises," I drawl.

Reece chuckles and sets his tablet on the side table. His frame easily unfolds from the chair, and he prowls toward the bed.

My stomach tightens with anticipation as a shudder races through my body, and I suck in a quivering breath. His broad smile fills in voids I didn't know existed. When he reaches the bed, he wraps his hands around my wrists and pulls me off the bed toward him. His mouth nuzzles against my ear. Warm breath wafts over the column of my neck.

"I can smell your arousal, pet." Teeth nip across the flesh of my throat and he releases my wrist. "It's intoxicating."

Under his touch I shiver. Inhaling a slow breath, I attempt to calm the rapid heartbeat and igniting flames racing through me.

I want to laugh. I want to cry. I want to beg for his touch.

Reece narrows his lust-filled eyes and stares down at me. Time slips into a lethargic pace. Around me, everything moves in slow motion. An unfamiliar warmth fills me. A languid peace covers me like a thick blanket of serenity. There is no fear in the recess and no clutter clouds my mind. Placid tranquility envelops me.

His arms wrap possessively around me as my head lolls against his shoulder.

A soft sigh escapes my lips. I close my eyes, savoring the touch of his strong hands sliding effortlessly across my back.

With a feral growl, his hand slides into my hair, gripping it. His lips slant over mine as his tongue plunges into my mouth in a demanding, urgent kiss. Greedily, I take everything he gives, a moan answering him. His hard cock presses against his pants. The fabric scrapes roughly against my thigh.

I wait in anticipation for his next move.

With a soft sigh, Reece hugs me to his chest.

"Please don't stop," I moan into his shoulder.

"Impatient as always." He chuckles. "You have no idea what you do to me."

Pushing away from me, he smiles.

"You are behind on your writing and I need to get work done, although you are far more tempting. Besides, lessons in patience are good for you." He smiles. "You'll find everything you need on the desk. Now get to work. I expect to see your thoughts when I am done with my own issues."

He kisses me lightly on the forehead and lets me go. I watch as he picks up his tablet and walks out of the room without a backward glance. My body hums with a palpable current as I watch his tight ass move through the doorway.

MY THOUGHTS ARE SCATTERED AS I WALK TO THE CLOSET. I TUG a pair of navy pants and a button-up shirt from the hanger, dressing as I move around the room. I let my mind wander on what I need to write. The words don't matter, but the sheer act of putting them to a page is a necessary practice. The last few months made it difficult to focus enough to even comprehend the effort. Now, as the world finds calm in the storm's eye, it is time to take the reins back under my control. Reece was right: writing was a perfect place to start.

He mentioned the fact my writing tools would be air gapped. That means no research or internet activities. I nod to myself in resignation of the lack of distractions and make my way to the desk.

A long silver-tipped feather fountain pen sits regally in its silver pen holder. Beside it, black, blue, and red inks sit in their bottles, neatly stacked linen paper between them. My eyebrows furrow at the sight. The elegant writing desk holds no drawers save one to the left. I rip it open, knowing this has to be a joke. Inside sits a small envelope with my name neatly written across it.

Picking it up, I pull the note from the envelope.

"YOU WILL FIND EVERYTHING YOU NEED TO WRITE. I'VE ENSURED *the best network security measures available. All of your supplies are air gapped by definition:*

Air gap—physically isolated from unsecured networks and electrically disconnected (with a conceptual air gap) from all other networks.

I've taken the liberty to ensure you have ample supplies for fonts, color changes and the ability to save documents or delete them and look forward to reading the end product.

~R"

I STARE AT THE PAPER AND PEN SET IN DISBELIEF. HOW CAN I possibly produce anything out of this ridiculous situation? Doesn't he know how much effort it takes to write in the first place and now he wants to hamper me with these primitive tools? Internally I rage.

My hands brace against the edge of the desk, the muscles in my body tensing and relaxing in time with my breathing. With a huff, I move the chair and sit down.

With a deep sigh, I move the stack of papers to the back of the desk and place a single sheet across the ink blotter. The movement has a ritualistic air about it. Removing the top from the black ink, I move it to the top middle of the writing space, place the paper on an angle and pick up the feather pen. Its balanced weight leans against my hand as I stare at the paper.

For a long moment, I stare at the blank page, willing words to form. Blankness shutters against my mind, but I dip the pen in the well anyway, then settle the tip against the paper. As if by magic, my mind opens and the pen moves across the page. The scratch of the nib against the linen paper is meditative. Within a few strokes, I refill the tip and continue the process. Words pour across the page. Fears, frustrations, and aggravation find a home as they embed into the linen. A feeling of accomplishment fills in as they pour out.

Page after page fills and I get lost in the process. My entire focus is centered on the process of pen and ink to communicate to no one but self. When my hand cramps, I stand up to stretch, surprised to see darkness outside my window.

"Productive day?" Reece's voice startles me. On the desk, a large stack of papers lies strewn. "Looks like I have quite a bit of reading to catch up on."

He nods toward the papers. "But right now, I want to feed you dinner."

"Feed me dinner?" Hesitation fills my voice.

"Yes. Now come."

THE WORDS RUN THROUGH ME. FOR HOURS I'VE PUT WORDS together on a page. Maybe I am being hypersensitive to syntax. Peace shatters as thoughts shove their way forward, each one evaluating the words, hesitating, weighing them through all my lenses and starting over. I frown at the flood of emotions and thoughts, agonizing over each and every one.

He leads us through the house to the terrace. We step down to the sunken seating area. The blue and red flames of the fire pit dance in the soft sea breeze scented with brine and herbs.

Beside me, Reece clears his throat.

The sound rips me from the sudden chaos of my thoughts. A hot blush runs over my cheeks. I look up into his gleaming eyes.

"Overthinking as usual, pet?" The corners of his mouth turn up as he smiles down at me.

"Busted."

He chuckles and wraps his arms around me. Here, nestled in the protective cage of his arms, I am safe. His gentle encouragement worked wonders on my battered confidence. Each step pushes me closer to the edge of my own world. It is a heady mixture of soft tenderness mixed with intoxicating demand. He was the missing piece in the mass duplicity of my world.

"Strip." The command is soft but no less demanding against the backdrop of the whispering waves.

He pushes me away and walks towards the long couch for a better view.

Torchlight highlights and shadows me. My hands shake with need and my fingers fumble down the buttons of my shirt. His gaze openly roams my body as I strip for him. It is like I can feel his bold stare rake against my skin in an open promise.

Where his gaze lingers, it ignites something in me I thought long dead. The wind stirs the waves of his hair, lifting the collar of his linen shirt against his jaw. His eyes narrow with each move of my hand, lashes meshing at the corners. I burn the image into my memory, the hard male contrasting with the soft white linen sculpting his body. A mix of demand and concern pushes me to the edge, ready to make everything right. With a deep breath, I steel myself for what he might have planned. One by one, the garments fall onto the terrace until I stand naked before him.

The breeze caresses my body like invisible fingers. It moves with the rise and fall of the sea as it runs across my curves. In response, my nipples pebble under the ghostly touch. Lust burns away the last of the internal chaos.

"Come."

Anticipation pulses through me as I move toward him until I stand in front of him.

"Hands behind your back."

My arms move until they cross behind my back. Reece stands and moves behind me, lashing my wrists firmly with a silk scarf. I luxuriate in the sweet sensation of being bound before him.

With an effortless grace, he moves back to the couch. Picking up a glass of ruby-colored wine, he drinks from it and appraises my body, sending shivers of awareness up and down my spine.

"Kneel." He points to the pillow on the deck between his legs.

With long unpracticed movements, I fold myself until my knees settle under me. My eyes fall to the floor. Every muscle in my body tenses with expectation and memories.

"Lean forward." The brisk command causes my head to jerk up.

The mask envelops my eyes. Darkness descends, blotting out all of the light. A hand pushes me back to settle against my heels.

CHAPTER TWENTY-TWO

MY EARS STRAIN for sound in the velvety darkness. The breeze off the water brushes through my hair, causing a shiver. Anticipation hovers on the edge of restraint. As I kneel at his feet, naked, bound and blindfolded, vulnerability and desire race through me.

The click of footsteps vibrates across the terrace, pausing suddenly as they step into the sitting area. A possessive hand lies against my shoulder. Dishes clang against one another, disturbing the serene night as the tray settles on the table to my left.

"Thank you, Timothy," Reece says above me.

"Sir."

The footsteps are much slower as he leaves than when he arrived.

"Calm yourself, pet. There's nothing here out of my control." A soothing hand brushes against my sensitive skin.

Above me, dishes clink together and draw my attention.

"Open." His finger brushes against my lip, and I open to him.

A warm cup presses against my mouth. The strong and tangy liquid flows over my parted lips. I savor each drop until the cup is removed.

Giving up this much control headily combines excitement and terror. For every bite I must trust him. With my body so vulnerably open, I must trust him.

His finger brushes against my bottom lip without a word. My mouth drops open in response. A garlicky aroma engulfs me, and I sink my teeth into the crusty thick bread. A moan of appreciation breaks the silence. When I swallow, his finger signals me again as the cool edge of the wine glass presses against my mouth. The bittersweet liquid melds in a perfect pairing with the garlic.

I'm lost in the bliss of the experience. Over and over, his finger softly signals me, and a new taste erupts across my tongue.

Sweet fruit juices run down my chin when the grilled pineapple explodes as I bite into it. Warmth radiates around me as he licks the errant juices away until his mouth owns mine. A breath catches in my throat. Fire races through me, straight to my core.

Reece pulls back, cupping my face.

"Still hungry?" His voice is hoarse with need.

"Yes. Please let me taste you." I groan and pull against the bonds on my wrists.

The words hang in the air. Above me, he stands, his thighs grazing against my shoulders. He moves with controlled impatience and settles back down on the couch.

His fingers knot in my hair and pull me forward. A finger runs across my lip and my mouth opens to engulf the soft tip of his cock. I lick away the salty fluid. A moan escapes against his rigid cock and his hand tightens in my hair.

With confidence, I take him farther into my mouth and work my tongue around the head in a steady rhythm. Under the sensitive tip, my tongue flattens, and he bucks forward with a growl.

I pause until he stills. A smile curls around my lips as I continue to work down his thick shaft in rasping stokes. I continue to move my mouth and lips, flicking his cock with my tongue and drawing back. Drawing in a deep breath, I exhale, letting the heat rush out in waves. His hips thrust, forcing his cock deeper into my mouth.

I move my head up and down his cock as I struggle against my bound wrists. With an effort, I pick up my pace with three fast strokes. His fingers tighten in my hair. He takes control of my movements, working my open mouth up and down his shaft. I gasp for air.

Above me, his body tenses. He pulls my mouth off of him and I struggle for balance.

"Atlas." His strained whisper grazes my ear.

An arm slides around my waist, drawing me into him before his mouth settles on mine. He tastes of heat and power. I open to his demands, needing more, as our mouths mesh. Each move makes my balance precarious until he steadies me again.

He pulls back. His body is still under mine, but his chest heaves as he works to find his own control.

"Own me, please." The words tumble unbidden as I give in to the moment in total surrender.

"Not in just this moment, Atlas. I want all of you." The words are deep and demanding, teetering on a dangerous edge. "No matter the mask you wear, I want to be the one beside you holding up your world."

"Yes." A strained whisper pushes out the words.

He stands with me in his arms and repositions my body until my ass is high in the air. The pull of my shoulders makes me strain under the position. He grips my ass with a hard squeeze.

"I want to see you struggle under your duplicity for me," he continues, his thumb sliding down the cleavage of my ass. "A plug firmly in your ass while you dominate a client on their knees."

His finger works across the edge of my pucker, and I push back against it in a groan.

"Or tight magnetic clamps reminding you of the pinch of my fingers while you discuss a client's next public relations campaign."

He leans over my body. His thumb and forefinger tease the taut bud of my exposed nipples, catching the left one and squeezing it in time with his words.

"Or bound under your dress at dinner, while I tease you mercilessly under the table."

I groan, remembering our first dinner together.

"No matter what, no matter where, no matter who you are in that moment... you are mine."

The dam in me breaks and the last vestige of pride falls in crumbling heaps at his words.

"Yes. Yours."

His fingers press inside my soaked pussy as his thumb circles across my clit. I moan in a combination of desperation and surrender. His words push me to the edge, and I crave each one. Fingers push into me, fucking me right to the edge until I am a squirming, panting mess, while his thumb presses against my ass.

"And when you need release, it is my hand which provides the pain and the pleasure." He lands three stinging hard smacks across my ass to punctuate his statement.

I know in my heart I want him in every way I can have him and will give him whatever he demands.

My hips drop in response to the pain and pleasure. I gasp when he breaches my ass. He pushes deeper into me and I spin in a spiral of sensations. Behind me, he groans and forces his thumb deeper. My ass burns at the invasion.

When he withdraws, I feel empty. I hear the faint crinkle of a wrapper.

"Open for me," he growls, the need in his voice obvious.

I relax and he breaches my ass once again while positioning his cock at the entrance of my soaked pussy.

"Beautiful."

"Please." The word strangles in my throat.

He shoves his cock into me in short, savage thrusts, mimicking the same movement with his thumb.

"Is that what you want, pet?"

I am full in every way.

"Yes!" I scream into the darkness and struggle against the bonds. "Fuck me! Take me. Possess me!"

WITH A HARD THRUST, REECE HOLDS HIS POSITION. MY BODY squirms in a demand for him to move. When I settle beneath him, my breaths come in desperate pants. The smell of him is intoxicating.

At last he moves, and the burning mix of pleasure and pain spirals through me in an explosive sensation. His cock thrusts into my pussy, only to withdraw while his thumb fucks my ass. I'm lost in a sea of sensation and clench down around his hard shaft. Above me, I hear the harsh intake of his breath and tight grunt as he pushes into me again.

My body clenches. An orgasm threatens to take me over and shatter every part of me. I try to focus and pant, my own primal sounds loud in my ears.

Suddenly, his hand fists hard in my hair. Reece crushes me down against the couch. The sea breeze whips around us, the salty tang in the air heightening the sensations in the dark. His cock pounds into me, jack hammering toward a desperate climax. I struggle against my own, trying to hold out just a little longer, the delicious friction penetrating every nerve.

"Please!" I beg with a strangled breath.

"Don't you dare come until I command it!" he threatens with a growl but doesn't let up his relentless pace.

My body writhes underneath him, riding through the overload of sensations. The thrusts in my ass and pussy throw me hurtling to a point I can't control. His words douse the inferno with gasoline until I am severed from all reality.

The punishing rhythm doesn't relent. Erotic oblivion threatens to send me careening over the edge as I fight to follow his command.

"I can't... " The words are strained. My voice sounds foreign in my ears.

"Come for me!" he roars behind me. His body slams deep into me, his cock pulsing as he gushes against the condom.

The words clip the last threads of control and I follow him over the screaming edge. The orgasm washes all reason from my mind. I thrash and moan as I plummet over the edge. I am vulnerably raw with need in its wake. My body collapses in exhaustion.

Reece doesn't move. His body still penetrates mine. His ragged breath tells me I am not the only one affected by what just happened.

With an effort, he untangles his hand from my hair. His thumb pulls out of my ass and I shudder. Reece pushes up and slides his semi-hard cock from my aching pussy. My heartbeat pounds in my ears and my shoulders scream in pain. I hear Reece move around me. The touch of a cool, damp towel makes me jump.

"Be still, pet. It's okay," Reece coos as he cleans between my legs.

The bonds on my wrist loosen and I groan at the sudden return of sensation as pins and needles race pain down my arms. Strong fingers press into the tight muscles in my back and shoulders. The slow massage pulls the pain from my exhausted limbs. When he is done, he picks me up and cradles my body against his firm chest. Here I feel safe.

I rock against him as we move through the house. The surrounding sounds change and, the sea grows faint. With care, he lays me on a soft mattress. It cradles my body and I give in to the exhaustion.

CHAPTER TWENTY-THREE

LIGHT SEARS MY EYES. A beam cuts through the deep sleep. A moan escapes. I roll over to avoid the assault and slam straight into a hard body. Everything freezes. My mind works to remember. Soft lips brush against mine. Hands wrap around my wrists and pin them above me.

My eyes fly open and stare straight into a pair of dark mischievous ones.

"Good morning, beautiful." His deep baritone voice resonates through his chest.

Without waiting for a reply, his lips work down my throat and the front of my chest until they wrap around the edge of the tight bud already forming. His tongue licks playfully right around the edges. My body pushes into his mouth and he devours the sensitive skin.

I cry out at the onslaught, but he doesn't let up. A taut, muscular leg wraps around mine, pushing his firm cock against my thigh. His mouth continues to work on its target. The heat of his body covers me as it radiates off him. The discord melts from my mind and I give in to the moment and the pleasure of his mouth on my breast.

"Please," I gasp.

The word makes Reece pause, and his head raises.

"Please what?"

"Don't stop," I unabashedly beg.

Reece chuckles.

I glare in response.

"You are beautiful when you give yourself to me." His other hand traces the down the curves of my body. The light touch tickles, and I jerk away. He lays his hand across my stomach. I am pinned by him with no effort on his part.

"Today we're getting out of the house," he says, his tone flat.

"You said this was the safest place."

"It is, but I've worked to ensure your safety elsewhere. You've been in hiding too long. It's time you stop running and fight."

"You don't understand..." Fear laces my voice.

"I do. You can't run forever. You are surrounded with people who will do whatever it takes to keep you safe."

"That's what scares me the most." The words are a whisper.

"It will be okay." His confident smile makes me want to believe him.

I nod, but there's no commitment behind it.

"Now, let's get your beautiful ass up and in the shower. I have a surprise planned for you today."

His hands release their grip on my wrists, and he rolls off the bed.

I openly watch his body. He moves across the room into the door to the right of the bed. Thoughts stutter. The bathroom in my room is to the left.

With a critical eye, I take in the room. The rising sun moves straight through the window. From the window, a grove of trees sways in the breeze. Every area of the room is decorated in local wood furniture and handmade objects. It stands in strict contrast to the clean modern arrangement of the guest suite.

Everything in this room is personal. Each object placed with pride. I stand and take it all in.

Reece peeks out of the bathroom door.

"Ogle my stuff later. Get your ass in here now." He grins.

REECE DISAPPEARS THROUGH THE DOORWAY. I HEAR THE shower turn on and follow. Waking up in his bed has me disoriented. Add it to the fact we are leaving the house and each step is one into the unknown. A place where all my control is lost.

I step through the partially open door and pause. My gaze is riveted on the large glass enclosure. His shower is large enough for three or four people. The warm water is steaming up the glass but not enough to shroud the shower completely. In fact, the steam adds to the mysterious look of the surroundings. Across the top is a large bar bolted into the wall and several other anchor points across the back. I smile at the last time we showered. The memories bring warmth back, chasing away the fear our conversation conjured.

"Atlas..." His voice was low, barely audible. My name brings me back to the present. There is a passion laced with concern in the tone.

"Yes, Reece?"

"Come here, pet." His hand pushes through the fog and I place mine in it.

The warmth of the shower engulfs my body when I step into it. Reece looks down at me, those dark eyes barely concealing his thoughts. Water rolls over the hard and soft features of his face. The dichotomy makes me pause and I want to reach out to touch him. I extend my hand to caress his cheek, but he catches my wrist.

Stunned, I try to pull my hand away, but his grip tightens.

"Careful, pet. You're in my domain, not yours. It may seem like a soft place, but there are hard edges which can cut and bite. A dark-ness you said you wanted to explore."

I yank my hand from his grip.

"If you are all that... bring it," I challenge.

His arm shoots out and wraps around my waist before I can move a muscle. In a flash I am pinned up against a wall with Reece staring down at me. This man is pure power. Nothing in him is restrained. His eyes flash between darkness and light. The promise of pain and pleasure. A place of hard and soft.

I know I should be frightened, but he is so commanding and sexy. In his arms I am safe and more turned on than I can ever remember.

My foot bumps against something heavy and soaked, but his gaze won't let me look away. His hand slides down my body, and something in me breaks.

"Reece." I moan out his name.

He wraps his hands under my ass and lifts me onto his hard cock. With one hard thrust, he pushes into me. My hands wrap around his neck as he kisses me hard.

CHAPTER TWENTY-FOUR

HE LIFTS his head and stares wildly down at me. Pinned under his gaze and by his body, I press into the wall. Then he dips his head and devours my mouth.

His tongue demands my response with a new level of urgency, nearly taking my breath away. Like a piston, his cock pounds into my body hard and fast. Each stroke in and out is driven by an unseen need. Our bodies slam against the dark marble tile, each movement smashing us against the surface. The pain of each smashing blow melds with the intense pleasure. The final walls of my resistance crash around me, and I meet his drive move for move. I cling to his wet body as much as he clings to mine.

Never have I felt so close to another soul in my life. The sex is hard, fast, and primal as we race toward release. All the frustration I've endured in the past few weeks explodes out of me. Here, he shares my anguish, fear, and loss of control. I reach for him like I've never reached for anyone before.

The primal level of our sex thrills and frightens me, but I only want more. I want him to fill me. The harder he pounds into me, the more I open to him. He groans into my mouth, driven by his own need to possess me.

A frenzy of pent-up release fills the air. His head lifts and he grinds out his release, forcing me over the edge. My body skids down the wet tiles as he slowly releases me from his grip. He holds my head to his heart as I sob out his name, panting softly against him.

Reece lowers me to the floor without a word. He watches my face. It contorts with all the emotions pouring out of me. He leans forward and presses his forehead to mine.

"You hold too much in," he whispers. "It takes far too much to empty it all out. Let the weight of the world go, pet. Let's bind you so we can lift together."

"I like the way you make me feel, Reece," I whisper.

His fingers graze across my lips.

"I'm with you." The words are simple, but their meaning makes me pause.

If he left me now, I fear I would truly be lost. I close my eyes and let myself enjoy his touch. His strong arms surround me as the water pounds across our skin. With an effort, I sit still, willing time to stop.

"I could sit here with you forever." His voice is barely audible.

I simply nod.

No matter the storm, once he understands me, he brings me back to center. Every time he speaks, I want to forget all the terrors in my world and only be with him.

The sodden end of rope snaking across the back of my neck brings me back to the present. Reece smiles down at me as he works it down across my shoulder and ties a knot right between my breasts.

HE LIFTS ME FROM THE FLOOR. IN EVERY WAY I AM NAKED before him now. My soul is bare. I am at his mercy. His hand guides the rope with an elegance born of long hours of practice.

"Arms above your head. Grab on to the bar. Do not let go," he commands.

Without thought, my hands reach up and wrap around the heavy metal bar. The move pulls my body taut and ready for him.

The rope flies through his fingers as it dances to his will. Each pull of the rope kisses and licks against my skin. Some moves are gentle caresses and others are stinging bites. He turns me, in complete control of my body, to wrap me in the tentacles of our connection.

He gazes down at me and I am awash with his power and focus. A shudder runs up my spine as the rope grazes across my sensitive nipples.

"Turn around."

I do as he bids, moving my hands only enough to reposition my back toward him. A fiery flash of pain explodes through me, then fades into the tightness of an embrace. His hands continue to tighten the lengths around my chest. Each wrap cinches my chest tighter until my breath comes in pants.

He pulls the rope until I am forced onto the balls of my feet. His power is palpable, and I breathe it in when his strong body presses against mine. Even in this precarious position, the assuredness he provides is unmistakable. Reece's hot breath nuzzles against my temple, and I push my head back to rest against his shoulder.

"Beautiful," he murmurs against my skin.

Water slides down his face and melds with the rivers flowing down mine. I close my eyes, enjoying his touch. He slowly lowers me back to my feet, and the rope once again flies through his fingers.

Each knot runs down the length of rope to the next, pulled together then separated apart, forming an intricate diamond pattern across my body while wrapping my breasts until they disappear from view.

A fast move pulls my focus as a knot lands against my clit and the rope slides along my aching pussy. The rope pulls and releases, and I moan against the racing sensations. He pushes away from me, and I stand free of his support.

"Let me see your eyes, pet." His hands push against my waist until I reposition and face him once again.

Under his heavy gaze, I shift and move in the binding ropes. It gently digs grooves into my skin. The knot across my clit applies a slow, even pressure. Each move makes me more aware of him. His touch is everywhere. My body sways in his rope's embrace.

"Let go of the bar." The command is gentle and firm.

His gaze shifts from my face. Hands grab me by the rope and he easily moves me. In one push, I am off-balance. With an easy assuredness, he pulls me back to center, proving his dominance and control. I surrender deeper to his protective power.

"Together, like this rope binds us, we can take on the world."

———

I AM TRANSPARENT TO HIM. UNDER HIS GAZE, MY SELF-consciousness rises. His finger runs across the knot pressing against my clit. His fingers continue until he once again deftly takes up the rope. It wraps tightly around my hips and between my legs until he is satisfied.

Reece leans me again the wall and turns into the shower's rushing waters. With his intense burning gaze away from me, I work to regain an even breath. My chest presses out against the ropes with an effort.

Glancing down, I see my body is covered in what can only be described as a wrapped bathing suit. I wonder at the mastery of art and devilish placement of knots. With the water no longer bathing us in warmth, I shiver.

A large towel wraps around my body and I look up to see a devilish smile play around the edges of Reece's mouth.

"It's time for an excursion," he announces, stepping out of the shower.

"An excursion?" I nearly stutter.

"Yes, pet. I told you we are getting out of the house today."

I look down at my body and back up to him, the question clearly written across my face.

"Don't worry, I have a cover-up for you. Trust. In every way," he says and leans down to kiss my forehead.

I watch him walk out of the shower and into the adjoining room. My hands move across the rope and send a thrill up my spine. For so long, everything in my world was controlled so tightly that the smallest thing was known. There I thought I'd found freedom in lifting my carefully built world. Yet here I stand, covered only in rope, about to embark on an excursion beyond the walls of this house.

Once again, Mr. Gabriel's mastery shines a light across my cracking world. A smile lifts around the corners of my mouth.

With the confidence of a new fawn, I step out on shaky legs. Arousal pulses through me and my body sings in the snug embrace of the rope.

I step into the sun-flooded room. Reece is dressed in a pair of khaki shorts and a teal blue polo shirt. He's slipping his feet into a pair of dock shoes when he notices my movements.

"Ready to face the world again, pet?" He grins.

I pull the towel tighter around my rope-covered body and lift an eyebrow.

"Yes. That is what you are wearing this morning, under this." He steps around the bed and picks up a dress along the way.

"Drop the towel, Atlas." His gaze sweeps across me as his fingers trail down the side of my face.

Unceremoniously, the towel falls to the floor. Reece chuckles. His hands make quick work of draping the sundress across my body. Then he drops to his knee and places a sandal on each foot.

"Let's go explore the world, Ms. Devereaux." He offers the crook of his elbow.

"You're incorrigible," I say and roll my eyes at him.

"You think this is incorrigible? The day is young and I'm just getting started." With that, he takes a step toward the door and I shake my head in his wake as I try to keep up with his quick steps.

CHAPTER TWENTY-FIVE

THE DRIVE down the coast is peaceful as Reece's hand lies gently on my knee. In the sky, the Caribbean sun brightens up the day in stunning glory. In front of us, a small van moves down the road in the same pattern. Behind us, another van follows. It is the first significant reminder of the security detail which surrounds me day and night here.

Fifteen minutes later, we pull into the top of the marina. Each vehicle pulls alongside the next. Around us, people mill about checking ropes and sails or drinking and socializing. I am suddenly self-conscious of the rope beneath my dress. Its bumps shape an indistinct outline through the fabric. I run a hand down my torso and sigh.

Reece squeezes my knee.

"I've got you." His full wattage smile melts my doubts a little, and I nod.

The door on either side of the car opens simultaneously. The large hand of the bodyguard helps me from the car, and I step out into the brilliant sunlight.

Reece rounds the back end of the car, smiling down at me.

"You look gorgeous," he murmurs against my temple, then takes a step back. "Shall we go sailing?"

"Well, that's definitely an excursion."

Beside me, Reece chuckles and takes my hand.

We wind through the docks of the marina with two bodyguards in tow. All around us, sails luff in the wind and the gentle tink of the halyards clinks against masts. At the end of a long dock, an inflatable tender sits with an idle motor.

Behind the wheel, a man nods at Reece in recognition.

"Shall we?" His hand waves to the small boat.

"This isn't a sailboat," I say dryly.

"Observant."

"Is there a reason it isn't docked in the marina?"

"Yes. I like this location, but she won't fit."

"There are fifty-foot sailboats all over this marina."

Reece simply nods.

"If I'd docked her at Christophe Harbor, she'd be a small boat too," he smirks. "Now, shall we?"

He hands me into the tender. At the bow, boxes of provisions line either side. Once I'm settled on the side of the large inflatable, Reece and the two bodyguards step in. The tender rocks hard under the shift, and I startle.

"Don't be afraid, Ma'am, she'll stay upright in far more violent situations than boarding." The captain smiles back at me.

Once everyone is settled, the two men onshore cast off the ropes. The captain deftly moves the tender through the marina traffic and picks up speed.

Reece's strong arms wrap around my waist, and I settle back against his hard chest. His fingers graze and pluck across the ropes hidden under my dress. The wind stings against my eyes but it is like flying across the water. I close my eyes and let the wind whip through my hair, breathing in the heavy salt air.

The boat slows and I open my eyes as we pull to against the back diving platform of the yacht.

"WELCOME ABOARD, MS. DEVEREAUX." A MAN IN WHITE shorts and a white button-down shirt beams at me and offers me a hand up.

Behind me, Reece steadies me against the rocking boat as jet skis buzz around us. Once I step onto the platform, the rocking ceases.

"Welcome back home, Mr. Gabriel." He turns to Reece when he steps in behind me.

"Thanks, Jack. How soon until we cast off?"

"As soon as the provisions are stowed, we can get underway."

"Just enough time for a quick tour." Reece turns and smiles.

I follow him through the open cockpit and into the cabin.

"She's huge," I whisper to Reece's back.

"She's only thirty-one meters."

"Only." I roll my eyes when he turns back around and shake my head.

A large saloon flanks us on the left with a U-shaped bench and table. Light spills in from the large skylights on either side of the large room. To the left, a large, well-appointed galley gleams in the sunlight, the stainless steel appliances shining like diamonds.

"This is the sailing yacht Escape from Reality. She's thirty-one meters long, or just under one hundred and two feet, if you prefer." He grins down at me like a kid with his favorite toy as he rattles off her dimensions and name. Pride radiates from him. "She was originally custom built for my grandfather in nineteen eighty-two. When I acquired her, she was in bad shape and is restored from the ground up with all the latest technology built into her."

"She's breathtaking." I glance around the cabin. The care and attention to detail is evident in every corner. The neo-classic design is the perfect blend of classic and elegance. In every cabin, sunlight pours in through well-placed skylights. The head in the master suite is tastefully done in gray marble, easily complementing the teak, white leather, and stainless accents throughout the cabin.

"Thank you," he says, pulling me through to the sleeping cabins. "She can sleep eight. There is a Master back here with its own head. A double and a bunk twin cabin for other members of a cruising party. Crew quarters are below. She normally sails with a crew of four, but this trip she will sail with six."

The words are supposed to assure me of my safety, but they only serve as a reminder that the surrounding threat is real. Still, I force a smile across my face. His enthusiasm is infectious.

Underneath our feet, the engines rumble to life.

"Let's go up on deck. You'll love the view of the island as we pull away from our mooring."

Reece leads me back through the small maze of rooms and back onto the deck. The crew focuses on each other as the anchor raises and they cast the lines off the mooring ball.

The yacht starts forward and cuts easily through the water under the motor's power. At the helm, Jack looks comfortable at the control and smiles as we pass.

We walk along the deck. His hand wraps around the ropes against my lower back, pulling the entire harness tight.

"Standby to raise the main!" Jack calls from the helm.

"Main sheet ready," comes the response from the crew.

"Raise the main," he calls back to them.

"Main sail made."

The large main sail climbs the mast in a steady rhythm. It is an awesome sight. As it reaches the top, it luffs in the wind.

"Stand by to bear away."

"Ready!"

"Bearing away."

The yacht moves and the sail fills. The sound of the motors is the only sound across the large boat. Hand signals and commands continue between the crew until three sails bend in the wind. With one last command, the engines die. Silence surrounds us. Only the lapping of the water against the hull breaks the serenity. The wind shifts and the sails luff, only to be pulled back into measure a minute later.

The large yacht cuts through the water effortlessly. I'm lost in the glorious freedom of flying across the water. In a trance, I move toward the bow of the boat and Reece releases his hold. I do not notice if he follows behind, but I'm drawn forward toward the sea and sit inside the bow pulpit. The wind flows around me, and my muscles relax, just taut enough to move with the pitch and yaw of the boat. Open ocean surrounds us as far as the eye can see. Here, a small dot in a grand sea, I finally escape from my harsh reality.

"Strip." Reece's command startles me.

"But the crew..." I start.

"Is my problem."

He helps me stand. I pull the dress over my head. My eyes dart toward the crew busy with various chores across the deck. In his left hand is a large bamboo rod, easily four inches in diameter. I eye it warily.

"My boat needs a figurehead," he states.

Beside his foot, a large bag of rope sits in a pile. A crewman hands him a large stainless rod and they fasten it into the deck. I note the grin they both share and tremble in anticipation.

"Stand on this box and face the sea," he says, nodding to the small square box in front of the pole.

I do as I'm bid. He grasps my shoulder and the rope snakes around my wrists, flying through his fingers. With a quick tug, my arms are jacked up behind me and cinched back down to the rope around my waist. His touch is cool and decisive. He knows exactly what he wants and is not willing to wait for me to follow.

The bamboo rod pushes through the opening of my arms, forcing my back to arch. He pushes me forward, and the bamboo rod catches against the steel. When he is satisfied, he bends down and pushes my feet together, wrapping the rope down both legs until it resembles a mermaid's tail. In a final flair, he wraps the rope around my hair and pulls it back to attach to the steel rod pointing skyward.

"Forward bend!" He issues the order.

The warm bodies surround me and the whole apparatus moves forward until I am at a forty-five degree angle to the water. Only the ropes secure me in position. Each one bites into my skin, forcing muscles to tense and release.

Reece walks in front of me.

"A beautiful figurehead for my ship," he says, gazing into my eyes.

My entire world sits in his hand. His strings push and pull my body as the yacht rolls through the waves.

His hand grazes a path down my body. Each touch sensitizes the skin underneath the rope. There's nowhere for me to hide. Arousal flames through me, and the heat of my embarrassment flushes across my cheeks. I can do nothing but accept his probing gaze across my body. The sweetness of being helpless before him washes over me.

"Mine," he whispers against my temple.

Between my legs, a low vibration buzzes against the ropes.

"I can't!" I hiss and wiggle in the rope.

"Oh dearest, you have no choice. You are caught like a mermaid aboard my ship and I will have my way with you."

The vibrator moves up my body. Every length of rope vibrates across me until I am consumed with need. Waves of pleasure crash over me, building my need toward a new rising crest. The boat rides high on a wave and crashes down on the other side, spraying us both with water, forcing Reece to move his hand.

"Looks like Neptune isn't ready for you go over the edge yet," he says with a wicked smile.

I strain against the bond, thrashing with the waves of pleasure and the bites of pain. Groans of disappointment and anticipation follow each move of the vibrator when he takes it away. I grind openly against the rope, begging the god of the sea for sweet relief. Over and over he pushes me to the edge of ecstatic agony. His power consumes me.

"Come for me, pet." The soft words break the last hold and my body quivers and thrashes against the ropes, giving in to the blind pleasure. As the wave crests, I expect the vibrator to stop, but he only presses it harder against the ropes, demanding the knot against my clit push me over the edge.

The pattern continues. He wrings the next orgasm from my body until I scream out in pain and pleasure. My body sags against the ropes.

Words surround me, but I do not comprehend them. Once again, they lift my body until the steel rod points skyward. The box is shoved under my feet and I sigh with relief. With care, he unwinds the ropes from my legs and works up my body. As my legs give out, Reece catches me in his strong arms and lowers me to the deck. Everything in me is disoriented and I sit naked, wrapped in his arms. A blanket engulfs me. I give over to the heady sensations coursing through my body.

"Drink," he commands and presses the water bottle to my parched lips. I drink like a woman lost in the desert. When I've had my fill, a smile creeps across my face.

"That was incredible," I murmur.

"From the height of mountains to the darkest parts of our souls, we share this journey together."

I nod and let the yacht rock my weary body to sleep in his arms.

CHAPTER TWENTY-SIX

THE GENTLE SWAY of the boat tells me we aren't moving. I stretch out the tension in my sore body. Rope bite marks line across my skin. Everything in me is at peace. My mind is still for the first time in far too long. It truly is an Escape from Reality.

I move toward the head and eye the shower. The saltwater from the earlier spray sticks like a crust on my skin and I give in to the indulgence. Warm water pulsates against the dents across my skin. My slick hands run along my body, the shower gel adding to the sensation. I think about the last few weeks and smile. In my chest, my heart pounds in anticipation of the next delicious adventure. Happiness fills me and I give in to it. I allow myself to revel in the joy of having this man in my life. The world is lighter, and the fear recedes to the darkest corners. With him I can take on the world.

Stepping out of the shower, I knot the towel around me and wince when it pulls against the rope bites. A jar of balm sits on the bedside table.

"Use generously. It will help with the ache. ~R"

The small handwritten note makes me smile as I twist off the lid. Dipping my fingers into the thick ointment, I smear it across my sore skin. Everywhere it touches, a line of fire follows in its wake until it calms to a slow smooth cooling burn. I force myself to apply the horrible cream across all the areas of my body until I am a mixture of fire and ice.

Picking up the cotton shirt, I glance at the bra. There is no way I'm going to put the bra against the rope abrasions. Sliding the fabric across my skin, I get dressed. The clothes are itchy and uncomfortable. Each layer adds a restriction I do not appreciate.

Wrapping my hair up in a knot on my head, I admire myself in the mirror. The hard peaks of my nipples push brazenly against the thin fabric of my shirt. Strands of hair fly out in all directions in a windswept look. I shake my head and eye the bra again. In a moment of defiance and need for comfort, I turn and exit the room.

The smell of garlic and herbs wafts in the air and my stomach growls in response. When I surface onto the deck, I'm met with the bustle of the crew preparing for our evening meal. Across the cockpit, Reece speaks into a satellite phone.

"Good evening, Devereaux," the captain says, and all eyes turn toward me.

Reece's head snaps in my direction, the heavy look of concern melting into delight as I step into the cockpit.

Beside me, a silver tray appears and the crewman smiles.

"Sundowner, Ma'am?"

"Thank you."

I pick up the cream colored drink from the silver salver and take a sip. A mix of rum and coconut rolls gently across my tongue. With enthusiasm, I take a large gulp.

"Careful there, killer," Reece says with a chuckle.

"It's good. What is it?"

"A painkiller."

I stare up at him with a look of disbelief.

"Seriously?"

"Yes. The crew thought you might need it after your rather long day." A wry grin pulls at the corners of his mouth. His eyes run down my body and pauses on the taut nipples pressing against the fabric.

"I like this look on you," he murmurs and ushers me toward the cockpit table.

ACROSS THE BOW, THE SUN SETS LOW IN THE SKY. SOFT WAVES lap against the hull of the yacht. In the distance, lights wink from boats in preparation for the setting sun. The soft clink of the halyard rings against the mast. The balmy evening is the perfect setting to the spectacular light show as the sun begins its journey down past the horizon. I swallow the last of my painkiller as the sun dips below the horizon and its last rays reflect across the dark sea.

Reece lays a firm hand against my back and steers me to the table. Once we are settled, a crewman pours both mineral water and white wine into the glasses on the table. From the galley below, Josephine appears with two beautiful plates. The fresh pasta makes the perfect bed for the seafood medley, topped with Parmesan and micro greens, drizzled in olive oil. I close my eyes and inhale the fragrant aroma of seafood, garlic, and herbs.

"You've outdone yourself, Josephine," Reece practically purrs.

"Stop sweet talking me, Mr. Gabriel." She smiles affectionately at him and disappears back to the galley.

We eat in silence, both lost in our own thoughts. I am concerned about the crease formed across Reece's brow but brush it aside. Under a hooded gaze, I watch him pick up his wine glass and savor the sweet elixir as it dances across his tongue.

"Thank you for today." The words are just a whisper on a breath across my lips.

"It was my pleasure, I assure you, pet."

I study his features in the dying sunlight. Shadows cast the perfect light across his face. This is the moment I want to hold on to forever. A quiet place where we just exist.

"Why the look of fear?" His voice is laced with concern and he lifts my chin with two fingers.

My words come out in a rush. "I don't want to screw this up. I know I'm a control freak and it complicates my world, but I'll do whatever it takes if you promise me you'll be right beside me."

I stare at him in disbelief of my words. I've never given them a voice before.

"I'm sorry," I mutter and try to force my head down.

"Why would I ever leave you, Atlas? I adore you." His voice is even and calm. "Ever since the day you walked away, getting you back into my arms was my one thought. Yes, some of your world shocked and frightened me, but the more you've let me in, I can see all the masks you wear. Each one we've removed together until your heart was revealed."

"I don't know how to fix this problem." I stare at my plate as tension fills my gut.

"We fix it together. The person with the least to lose always has the upper hand, but you have an entire team of people who want nothing more than to even the playing field. Let us."

"You don't understand."

"Then make me understand."

"He threatened to take away everything I hold dear. There's 'ownership' within a dynamic relationship and then there is owner-ship in the real sense of the word. Edmund won't be happy until he gets the latter."

"I thought he was your submissive. He paid you professionally."

I nod as I remember our many quiet sessions together.

"At the end, he wasn't satisfied enough to share me with the rest of my world. He asked me to marry him and I refused. Shortly after, he threatened me. Each one was stronger than the last. Every person around me was in jeopardy. I wouldn't be surprised if the story in the newspaper was because of him."

The shock I expected from Reece never comes. He sits quietly across the table and listens.

"We need to go back, Atlas. We can't run forever. Your world needs you to lift it again."

I shake my head. "I can't. I'm not ready."

"I wasn't asking if you were ready. I was informing you of the plan. We'll spend two more days out at sea. Tomorrow we'll snorkel and sail. Then we'll sail back to the marina. The security team is already in motion and packing to head back."

Stunned, I start to argue.

"Don't. You've done it your way and we are no closer to resolution. It's time to do it our way." His tone brokers no argument. "Now come here."

I sigh deeply and move next to him.

His arms curl around me and pull me up against his hard body.

"Now, did you wear this shirt without a bra to drive me crazy or the crew?"

I look up and smile mischievously.

"The world may never know, Mr. Gabriel."

"Trying as always, Ms. Devereaux."

"Maybe you should tangle with Alexandra instead." I smirk.

"I'll be glad when I see her again. She'll do you some good."

He kisses the top of my head and we watch the last lights of the dying sun.

HIS HAND MOVES ACROSS MY SHOULDER AND DOWN THROUGH the opening of my shirt, weighing and caressing my breast. He does not rush his movements. Feather touches glance across the tip of my hardened nipple, and my head falls back onto his shoulder.

A crewman steps into the cockpit and glances over at us. I shift in embarrassment, but Reece pinches my nipple hard to hold me in place.

"Good evening, Josh," he says casually, as if our compromised position is the most natural thing in the world.

"Good evening, Mr. Gabriel. Ms. Devereaux."

Josh turns and cleans up the table from our scrumptious dinner.

"Josh, may I ask you a question?"

I tense in Reece's arms.

"Of course, Mr. Gabriel."

"Did you find Ms. Devereaux's attire distracting in the cool evening breeze?"

I don't even need to look to know there's a wolfish smile painted across Reece's face.

"She's dressed quite lovely, Mr. Gabriel." Josh smiles back, but there's something in the way the two men communicate without words.

Josh nods, picks up the plates and silverware, and disappears down the hatch.

"Atlas, come straddle me with your back toward my chest," he whispers and plants a kiss on the edge of my temple.

Nervousness washes over me. I look around us and peer into the inky darkness, well aware the lights in the cockpit clearly illuminate us.

"Trust."

I nod and sit up. Beside me, Reece moves to accommodate his request. I lift my right leg over his lap and settle back against his chest.

"Grip the edge of the table and do not let go, or I'll flip you over said table and give you a spanking in full view of the world."

"Yes, Sir," I whisper.

A thrill runs up my spine at his authoritative tone. His assuredness is my anchor.

I lean forward and grasp the table's edge. My thumbs lie against the top while my fingers clamp it underneath.

Reece shifts behind me. His arms reach out, and his fingers begin to work the buttons down the front of my shirt. As each one releases, the sea breeze adds its own caress. He continues until only the last buttons hold the two sides of the fabric closed. Then his hands move to my shoulders and pull the shirt down to my elbows. The last button holds the fabric bondage in place.

Satisfied with his work, he plants featherlight kisses down my spine. His hands mold my breasts to fit into his palms. Lifting his head, he presses his hard body against me, tugging and rolling each nipple between his thumb and forefinger. A shiver runs through my body and my hips push forward against his lap.

Footsteps from the hatch draw my attention straight up, and my breath catches.

Josh is standing halfway up the hatch, staring appreciatively in our direction. My grip on the table tightens. I let my head fall forward in an effort to hide from his gaze.

"Look up, Atlas. You have an admirer," Reece says in my ear.

He releases one nipple and entangles his hand in my hair, forcing my head up, my back to arch and my breasts to jut out between the fabric of my shirt.

CHAPTER TWENTY-SEVEN

JOSH GLANCES down at the deck.

"Please, Josh, it's okay. She's beautiful," Reece says from behind me.

With a smile, Josh looks up and watches as Reece's fingers continue to caress and plunk my nipples.

"Aye, she is gorgeous," he replies appreciatively.

"I thought it was unfair how she teased the crew with just a hint of the beauty beneath."

Josh nods and swallows hard.

"I haven't seen the captain this evening. Is everything okay?" Reece asks with concern.

"The captain and the other crew seem to have a touch of food issues. They should be okay by morning."

"Nothing serious, I hope."

"It is just some discomfort."

"Yet you are fine?" Light suspicion laces his voice.

"Aye. I'm a vegetarian. My provisions come from the main house. Josephine normally supplies all of our meals, but the crew picked up some local provisions from the market today."

Reece nods. His hands continue to work on my breasts and slide down my stomach to the edge of my shorts. Josh's eyes follow the move of his hand until it disappears under the table.

"Is there anything else I can get you?" Josh asks, stepping to the table and picking up the remaining glasses.

"Please make sure there is water in the main berth," Reece replies without missing a beat.

"Aye, Sir. Please ring if you need anything."

"Thank you, Josh."

"Thank YOU, Sir."

Josh beams, nods in my direction, and turns toward the hatch, disappearing down the stairs.

Reece releases my hair. My breath comes in a shutter as my head falls forward. His fingers push past the waistband and between the lips of my pussy.

"I believe the lady doth protest too much," he whispers against my ear.

"Why? Why did you do it?" I croak.

"In this place, you are mine. Together we explore the darkness and the light. Step out of comfort zones and find a life behind those masks you wear."

"So you want to share me?" The words are an accusation.

"I don't share, Atlas." It is a definitive statement.

"But..."

"Your body is beautiful, and I wanted to show it off. Besides, you were teasing the crew."

"Most men are possessive in these situations."

"Then they are not confident in their place nor in their level of control."

"And you are?"

"I am. You are mine. All of you. Every mask you wear belongs to me. Just as I belong to you. It is a symbiotic relationship. I give you a place to hand off your world and you give me a place where I can let my darkness out of the cage without fear. Here we give each other what we need, want and desire."

The words melt through me. Everything I need to lift the world is right here with me. A smile breaks out across my face.

"I can't wait to see how you handle Alexandra and Atlas on a daily basis." I turn my head and grin back at him.

"Oh, I think I will enjoy Alexandra and her superior, haughty attitude the most."

"She is not haughty," I snap.

Reece chuckles.

"Just imagine, under that tight business suit, five-inch heels and perfect makeup, a pair of magnetic ball nipple clamps. The pain and numbness over a few hours racing through her body as she dominates her clients and keeps her staff in line."

My breath catches at the image.

"Or Atlas sitting in her PR firm, with a butt plug deep in her ass controlled by me across her phone. Not knowing if it will go off when she's on the phone with a client or out on a business call."

"You wouldn't."

"Yes. I will. Small reminders that I know exactly who and what you are to me."

"But what if someone finds out?"

"Then you best up your game and make sure they never do."

Arousal rushes through me on the heels of my trepidation. His fingers push into my soaking pussy, and I gasp.

"Days when your ass is sore, you will pace your office because it will be more comfortable than sitting down. Or a tight rope harness just under your business suit with a clit knot pulling tight against this..." He pinches my clit hard to punctuate the word and I nearly come.

"Oh, God," I pant.

"Locking the door to Alexandra's office and fucking you hard across her desk, unable to make a sound because your assistant is just right outside. While you hope you turned off the cameras so your security detail doesn't get a show."

He pinches my nipple hard and pushes two fingers just inside me.

My mind is in overdrive. All thoughts of my surroundings vanish in his words, each scenario playing across it like a movie. The logistics of them are verified and turned into realistic fantasy in seconds.

"Seeing you kneel at my feet at the end of a long day, begging for my mark. Begging for your release from holding up the world. Willing and waiting for me to provide you a haven in every way you need. Not through hearts and softness but through roses and thorns."

His hard cock presses between the cheeks of my ass. I rotate my hips back and move them forward across his hard length. He groans in response.

"Two can play at this game, Mr. Gabriel."

"About time you showed up, but if you move your hands, you know the consequences."

I lift off his lap, and he pulls his hand from my shorts.

"If this was a skirt, I would demand you unzip your shorts and push my hot wet pussy down onto your hard cock. Right here in plain sight, without anyone noticing anything but the movement of two bodies."

I let my body slide up and down with my words.

"When it is deep inside, I would settle on your lap. Letting my muscles squeeze against your hard length but refusing to move, so as not to draw too much attention from the crew."

His hands clamp down on my hips in response, and he pulls me down into his lap.

Sharp teeth bite deep into my shoulder. Pain flares across me, and I moan against it. When he releases my shoulder, he licks across the teeth marks.

"Mine."

As a unit, we move to the edge of the bench.

"Let go of the table, Atlas."

My hands unclasp from the table and are immediately engulfed in his as he moves toward the hatch and down the stairs.

CHAPTER TWENTY-EIGHT

WE REACH the master berth and he spins me toward him. He stares into my eyes while his fingers ease down the zipper of my shorts, then he tucks his thumbs through the edge of the waistband and sends them south.

"Sit," he orders.

I move to the bed and sit on the edge. Reece kneels between my legs and leans in to kiss my inner thigh. He works his way up my leg and skips my sex, then trails kisses down the other thigh. When he's done, he travels the same route, this time nipping the skin gently. My hips rise in a silent plea when he skips my sex again.

He moves his attention along each lip of my labia, licking and nipping without rush. I moan and relax under his tongue. He stands up and moves my shirt until it tangles around my elbows. With a decisive move, he ties the ends of the shirt hard in place. My hands fall behind my head, but I am truly bound under his command.

A moan of frustration escapes my lips, and he smiles down at me.

"Patience, pet."

My body tilts toward him when he once again kneels in front of me.

He leisurely slides his tongue back along the sensitive skin, making circles around my clit until he flicks it right across the top. I freeze, fearing any move will send me crashing over the edge.

His finger skims the edge of my entrance. In a simultaneous move, his tongue assaults my clit as he slides his finger deep inside. My hips buck in response and the muscles tighten around his finger. He works his finger and tongue faster. Right on the edge, he stops and pulls his finger back.

"Nooo! Don't stop!" I demand, frantic with need.

"You aren't the one in control, pet. Imagine sitting on the edge of your desk in this situation, when I stop right as your orgasm threatens to overwhelm you and simply walk to let you get on with your day."

"You wouldn't!" I shriek.

"Yes, I will."

His lips catch my clit and suckle it gently as he shoves two fingers in and moves them with a deep rhythm. With each stroke he adds to my torture. The last vestige of my control evaporates in his hands.

"All of those things and more. Please," I beg for all the images in my head.

"Please what, pet?" His head lifts long enough to issue the words before he starts his sweet torture again.

"Fuck me please, Sir. Make me yours!"

"Make you mine, pet?"

"Yours." The word is true.

Reece picks me up and tosses me higher on the bed. The bondage around my arms pulls against sore muscles. The soft movements are gone. Pent-up tensions are on the edge for both of us.

"Open yourself." He looks down at me. My legs part as he undresses. He crawls onto the bed between my legs and leans over to the nightstand, swiftly opening the drawer and pulling out a condom. He rolls it down his hard shaft and my entire body quivers in anticipation.

"Don't take your eyes off of me. If they close, I will stop. No matter how much you beg, I will leave you here to lie in your own need."

"Yes, Sir."

He grabs two handfuls of my ass and lifts my hips toward him. The first touch of his cock to my entrance makes me arch off the bed. He doesn't move, but I squirm and lift, trying to end my suffering.

"I can stay right here all night. Or you can surrender and let me lead."

My breath comes in pants and I force my body to still.

IN A CONTROLLED MOVE, HE SINKS INTO ME. I CLUTCH AND tighten around him. My eyes take a long blink.

"Eyes on me," he growls through clenched teeth, proving his control is on the same tight tether as my own.

I stare back up at him.

"I surrender."

Reece pulls out and rams into me. Each move uses my body until it follows my words. I tense under him and give in to the uncontrollable orgasm as it washes over me. He forces himself deep inside as my pussy clamps down around him and bends toward me.

"You didn't ask permission to come, pet. I own those too." His tone is like an iron fist in a velvet glove. Perfectly controlled and right on the edge.

He bites down hard on the soft skin between my neck and my shoulder.

"For every action or inaction, there is a consequence."

My body ripples around him. Nonsensical words pour from me.

He pulls out roughly and grabs me hard. In one quick motion, I am face down. I try to scramble to my knees, but his hand pushes against my back, pressing me into the bed. He thrusts his cock back into me and rams it across my g-spot.

Fisting his hand in my hair, he pulls me back and balances on the bed with his other hand. With each stroke I want to cry out for more. This, this is exactly what I want from him. A place where I can just be his.

I cry out every time he bottoms out but nothing in me wants him to stop. If only he'd rip the condom off and mark me truly as his. I try to put the thought down for a later discussion, but it evaporates as quickly as it forms.

Here I am completely at his mercy and I love everything about it.

"Come for me, Atlas," he grinds out behind me, slamming hard into me.

Every muscle in my body tenses under the command as my pussy spasms and milks him. Inside, his cock pulses and quivers as his body rushes over the edge of ecstasy. Aftershocks ripple through both of us.

When our bodies calm, he leans down and presses his lips on the back of my neck. Gently, he pulls out of me and disposes of the condom. When he returns, he rolls me onto my back and unties my arms.

I blink wildly when he brushes the hair out of my eyes. His finger trails down the side of my face and neck. A shiver runs through me at his touch, and I moan in response.

"Are you okay?" he asks as his arms wrap around me. His lips descend against mine in a light kiss.

"If feeling like I'm standing in the sun, open and free is all right, then yes, I'm okay."

"It sounds like exactly how I feel when I'm with you."

For a long time I lie in his arms until our breathing returns to normal. I want to stay right here forever, and I let my heavy eyelids close as I bask in the glow.

"Before you go to sleep, let's get you in some pajamas," he whispers against my ear.

"But I thought you liked me naked and available."

"Oh, I do. It is a matter of practicality on a boat. Better to be prepared than caught with your pants off." He smiles against my cheek.

"Quite practical, Mr. Gabriel."

"It's a matter of protecting what is mine, Atlas."

"Yes. Yours."

He shifts away from me. Once he's up, he steps to the dresser and pulls out a pair of pajama pants and a T-shirt.

Without a word, I pull them on.

Across the room, I watch him get dressed in his early clothes.

"Aren't you coming to bed?"

Reece steps around the foot of the bed and bends down to kiss my forehead.

"I need to check on the crew and make sure they are okay. If a couple of them are down with a bug or food issue, they may need a hand with the night watch."

I want to pout like a child, but this is the mantle of leadership, and I know it well. So I simply nod.

He pulls down the covers and waits until I settle into the bed.

"I'll hold you in my arms soon. Sweet dreams, pet."

My eyes close in exhaustion as I watch him walk out the door.

CHAPTER TWENTY-NINE

LIGHT SEARS MY EYES.

An intense beam of light cuts through the deep sleep.

A moan escapes and a hand clamps hard over my mouth.

My eyes fly open and stare straight into a pair of dark, sinister ones.

"Hello, Mistress." His deep cultured voice resonates through the cabin.

Without waiting for a reply, a knife works down my throat and the front of my chest. The sharp edge trails down the sensitive skin, leaving a light trail of blood in its wake.

I cry out against his hand. Fear and pain overwhelm my senses, but he doesn't let up. A taut, muscular leg wraps around mine. The knife continues to work its way across my tender flesh. The heat of his body is in sharp contrast to the cold dampness of his wetsuit. The discord screams through my mind.

"Please," I gasp when his hand moves to give him a better angle.

The word makes Edmund pause.

"Mistress, it isn't becoming of a Dominant to beg. Though it is a well-known fact the submissive has all the power. It is time you learn who is actually in control here and time for you to come home with me."

"Where's Reece?" I croak out.

"Sleeping it off with his buddies, I guess," he snarls.

Fear races through me. The very reason I ran was to protect everyone I loved. I thought this nightmare couldn't possibly be real. That I was strong enough to fight back and take control of my world. Here in the darkness, face to face with it, I crumble.

"It will be so perfect, Mistress. Knowing I will fall to my knees and crawl to you at the end of each exhausting day. To suffer under your exacting expectations. The constant demand for perfection in each move to serve you." A dark look intermingles with the fantasy in his head, lighting a spark in my own.

"I command you to let me go, boy." I fight the nausea rising in my stomach, pushing a firm, exacting tone through my lips.

Edmund laughs.

"You command me? After I've worked so hard to bring you back to me? All the things I've done to make you look my way? When you told me no after so many years of perfect service? You command me to let you go now?"

He shakes his head. "Don't you know, Mistress, it is the submissive who enjoys all the power in the relationship? I gave you that gift, and you threw it in my face when I asked for it to only come from me. Let you go?" He whispers the harsh words between clenched teeth. Each one is punctuated by the knife pushing into my skin.

A stream of blood runs along the rope bites down my chest.

"Now look what you've made me do, Mistress." Edmund sighs and grabs a towel. "If you'd just accepted my offer, no one would have gotten hurt. Their pain, suffering, and blood are on your hands."

He swipes at the blood, but it only reappears seconds later.

"It's time to go. You left a note this time. Since you've already disappeared once, I'm sure no one will care. They are all tired of this cat-and-mouse game as much as I am. I thought you were stronger than this nonsense, but in my home I will lift your agonizing world from your shoulders. You will have no cares, other than to command your servant and live in the lap of luxury."

Edmund wrenches my arm behind my back and forces me to my feet.

"Scream and I will cut your spine in two. Not just severing it but making you dependent on someone for your every living need."

Anger mixes with the fear at the bastardization of everything I know. I nod in acquiescence.

His tall frame half drags and half carries me through the yacht and up into the cockpit.

———

"WHEN I KNELT IN FRONT OF YOU AND ASKED FOR YOU TO marry me, I would have done anything to make you happy. But you rejected me without thought or comment. Since then I've watched a so-called Dominant become a weak, pathetic woman." His words are like ice cold water dripping from his lips.

"You know nothing," I spit.

"I found you in the middle of the sea, didn't I?" He sneers.

"How?"

"It is simple really. When one can attack, they must seem unable; when using one's forces, they must seem inactive; when one is near, they must seem far away; when far away, one must seem near," he hisses against my ear as he pulls me through the gallery.

"*The Art of War*," I whisper under my breath.

"Of course you know it, yet you never apply its lessons. Sad really," he huffs. "You are stupid and pathetic for a woman who is well educated. One I used to think was strong."

He looks at me with a mix of awe and disgust.

My eyes drop to the floor. The small trail of blood through the galley makes my heart stop. The entire boat is shrouded in the silence of a tomb on the water.

"Then why do you want me?" I challenge softly.

"Because I can't get enough of you. When you sat on the throne during our sessions, all I wanted to do was kiss your feet and provide your every need on a silver platter. Imagine my surprise when I discovered your little ritual in Boston. Dominick was quite helpful to the last."

My heart stops in my chest. The words twist slowly and painfully deep, lacerating me until it feels I'm already cut in two. Dominick's face flows through my mind, his demanding voice ringing in my ears.

"Enough talk. Move." He drags me painfully up the stairs and into the cockpit.

Edmund presses the knife into my back, and a wave of nausea washes over me. I force a deep cleansing breath into my lungs and the wave passes.

Out on the deck, the night is peaceful. Light waves lap at the side of the boat. Splatters of blood look like a Pollack painting across the pristine white deck, and I gasp.

"It's your fault, you know." Edmund's head nods to the blood spatters. "I warned you everyone would pay for your sins, just like Eve caused humanity to pay for her weakness."

"If I go with you, will you leave everyone else alone?"

"Mistress, I've promised that from the beginning, but the blood of some..."

Tears threaten to spill as my heart wrenches at his words.

"But there's still hope for the others," he says brightly and loosens his grasp on my arm.

Inside I scream as the implications tear through me in terror, but this ends now. I take a deep breath and pull every ounce of courage forward.

"Edmund—" The authority in my tone reflects confidence I do not possess. "If this is how you treat your Mistress, then you aren't worthy to kneel at my feet or anywhere near them."

My tone shifts something in him, and he turns to face me.

"WELL, WELL," HE WHISPERS WITH A REVERENCE.

For a long moment he stares at me. His fingers trail softly down my face. I want to jerk away, but I let my eyes harden instead.

"I don't believe you asked permission to touch me, boy," I reply in a superior tone.

Like a precious jewel, he evaluates me. He gazes down at my form and back up into my steely eyes.

"Attack him where he is unprepared, appear where you are not expected," he quotes softly. "Maybe you learned your lessons, just too late in the game to matter. While you were playing chess, I was playing the game of Go. My king is still well fortified, and I have surrounded more territory than you."

A brief smile crosses his lips.

"In case it is unclear, Alexandra, I am winning. You want to be owned? Believe me when I tell you, I own you far more than anyone else on this Earth. From here on, you are mine to control. When I give you something, you will be forever grateful, or I will inflict suffering to bring you quickly in line. The commands may come from your precious beautiful lips, but they will be the words I desire."

"The Dominant holds the power and the control," I challenge.

"If you were a real Dominant, the situation would not have come to this, but we both know you aren't."

The words shield the softest parts of me. In this moment I am glad of his malice. It gives me something to hold on to in the darkness.

"When you are bound and feel the bite of my whip against your soft skin, bleeding under each bite," I say, stepping into him, "then we shall see who wields the power. Your sharp, ungrateful tongue or my whip."

I hold my breath. It is a dangerous move and I wait for his reaction.

Edmund stares at me. Around us, the air is thick. Neither of us gives up ground.

"Welcome back to the game, Alexandra. You've got some major ground to make up in our little tête-à-tête."

He grabs my arms and spins me around. The knife point presses against my back as it slices through the fabric of my shirt. A warm trickle of blood traces its way down the hollow of my spine.

Letting go of my arm, his hand wraps forcefully in my hair, and he lifts me until I am forced to stand on my toes. I clamp my eyes shut and still my body. With force, he throws me down until my knees slam against the deck. I fall forward onto my hands.

A sticky slick substance coats them. The wetness penetrates the fabric over my knees. I force my eyes open and stifle a scream.

Edmund's foot presses against my shoulder blades until I am flat against the deck, the puddle of blood soaking into the front of my pajamas.

"Their blood is on your hands, Alexandra. Remember the consequences of your decisions."

CHAPTER THIRTY

EDMUND PULLS me up by the hair, and I struggle to stand.

He marches me toward the bow of the yacht. With each step, the trail of blood gets wider. As we approach the bow pulpit, I see a body slumped against the standing rigging. There is no movement.

"Noooo!" I scream as I recognize Reece's form, blood pooling around him.

"Looks like everyone is dying to be in your world, Mistress. Two down, one to go."

The shocking implication slams into me.

I twist in his harsh grip and ram an elbow hard into his stomach. His hand lets go in response and I run to Reece. My knees skid painfully across the deck when I get near him.

"Reece, please don't die on me. You promised!"

A shadow looms above me and I turn to look up at Edmund. His dark sinister eyes no longer shine with the bright elegance of the man who once knelt before me.

"This is your own fault. No one else to blame but yourself for these unnecessary situations," he says calmly.

"No." I choke on fear like a fist down my throat, willing Reece to move.

At the other end of the long yacht, I can hear a barely audible voice in the cockpit.

"Mayday, mayday, mayday! I say again, mayday, mayday, mayday! This is the yacht Escape from Reality, we are under attack. Entire crew is injured!" Fear and determination mix in the faint voice.

"We are latitude 17.307415. Longitude -62.623999."

Edmund looks at me with a hostile glare as the situation rapidly changes around us.

"You can choose me or you can be alone, Mistress," he snarls.

His cruel words hit like bullets.

"Until you are mine, Alexandra, your world will be a living nightmare and I will take all you hold dear from you." His cold, harsh voice rips through me.

He throws the large bloody diving knife at me. It embeds into the boat deck beside my thigh, grazing the edge.

"You want a war? I'll give you a war. I am not your possession. You are not my nightmare. This ends now!"

I pull the knife from the deck and throw it with all the raging emotions.

Edmund groans as it embeds in his shoulder. His eyes go wide as he stumbles backward at its force. The lifelines do little to assist him, and I watch him tumble over the edge.

I crawl to Reece's body. Large pools of blood surround him. Despair twists and turns inside me.

"Don't you dare leave me, you promised! I love you."

All I want is for him to look up at me.

"Don't make me do this without you. Please open your eyes and tell me you love me," I beg.

I cradle his limp body against mine. His breaths are harsh and shallow as I will his chest to move up and down.

Tears flow freely down my face. With a deep breath, I lay his head on the deck with care.

I rip off my shirt and look across his body for the largest wound. Dark red stains the left leg of his shorts, and a smaller stain creates a ring on his right shoulder. With determination, I crawl to his leg and push up his shorts.

Blood flows freely from the large open gash. I gasp at the damage. The cool night air brushes against my bare skin, but it barely registers as I fold the shirt into a large square and press down on the artery.

Reece moans.

"Don't you dare die on me, Reece Gabriel! I forbid it. Do you hear me?" I scream.

"I love you too, pet." His words are barely a whisper.

"You can't let him win." My voice shakes under the weight of the words.

"You need to go home, Atlas." He forces the words through his lips in a labored breath. "You are stronger and safer there. Please don't fight me on this one."

A ghost of a smile hints around the edge of his lips.

"It'll be okay."

His breath pauses, and his head lolls against the deck.

A howl looses from its moor deep in my soul.

"You can't leave me!" I scream. "You promised!"

Desperate tears spill in rivers down my cheeks as sobs wrack through my body.

In the distance, the whomp of helicopter blades cuts through the silence. The faint sound of motors floats on the breeze.

My mind focuses only on Reece as I roll him on his side, pull his leg forward, and tilt his head back.

Mast lights wash everything around me in the same brightness as daylight.

Heavy boots thud against the deck in a rush.

"They are over here!" a man shouts, and the thud of another set of boots vibrates across the once beautiful teak.

When they arrive, I am lost in a sea of numbness, my hands firmly planted on Reece's thigh.

A heavy bag lands with a thud on the deck.

"Ma'am, I'm a trained medic."

The man's strong voice pulls me out of my helplessness.

My head jerks up with unseeing eyes.

"Ma'am, you've got to let him go."

My head shakes vehemently from left to right. If I let him go I might never see him alive again. I want to demand this nightmare to end, to rewind the day to when I was captured in his strong arms. Under me, his skin grows cool.

"I can't help him if you don't let him go."

Strong hands disentangle my body from Reece's long, limp frame. A blanket wraps around my shoulder, and I'm ushered back toward the cockpit.

All around me, chaos erupts in the night. Tenders pull up to the back of the yacht.

My throat closes in grief. Air refuses to enter my body as I struggle to breathe. Sorrow and guilt consume me. The weight is almost too much to bear.

A crushing wave of despair threatens to drown me as I watch an army of people swarm the yacht. Ropes stream down from the sky as a helicopter hovers overhead. Hands communicate wordlessly. The oppressive downwind of the helicopter above only adds to the crashing wave of despair.

CHAPTER THIRTY-ONE

MY BARE FEET pad back through the blood on the deck, leaving red footprints in my wake. The entire scene is surreal.

"Ma'am, you should go shower and dress. There's nothing more you can do you here."

I stare at him for a long time. The words refuse to penetrate the fog of my shock. My body shivers.

"Ms. Devereaux." A woman's voice cuts through the night. "Let's get you cleaned up and dressed, Ma'am."

My head drops and I stare at my bloody feet and look back up.

With a nod of understanding, she disappears into the hatch and returns with a towel. Dropping to her knee, she taps my foot, and I lift it. The cold, damp fabric brushes roughly against the sole of my foot. When she taps it again, I automatically set it down. A dry towel covers the deck as it pokes into my foot. With a tap on the other foot, the process is repeated.

When both feet are clean, she places her hands on my shoulder and steers me toward the hatch. My movements are automatic as we move through the yacht. She does not stop in the main berth but continues to the attached head, steering me from behind. Once we step inside, she turns on the water.

"Take your time, Ma'am. I'll lay out some clothes for you." She turns and leaves when I don't acknowledge her. The door shuts with a soft click.

I stare in the mirror at my blood-covered clothes until steam fogs the mirror and the image disappears from view. With robotic movements, I peel away the sticky fabric and step into the warm shower.

Everything is heavy. Water stings the abrasions on my hands. I slowly take stock of my injuries, recounting how I obtained each one. My scalp hurts, my wrists are sore, and my knees throb. My mind wanders to thoughts of Reece. A deep shudder runs through me as tears prick my eyes. Without warning, my stomach convulses, and I drop to my knees.

The water under me runs red. With each passing second, it begins to fade until it is clear once more. All I want to do is curl up in a ball and demand the world go away, but I've been running long enough. Running is what brought me to this point. Running is what spilled the blood I watched pour across the deck. The running stops now.

I push up from the floor and box my emotions. There will be time for release later. Now it's time to get back to work. Time to end this insanity. I scrub my body until my skin is raw.

Everything in me tries to will the fog away, but it refuses to lift. I step out and wrap a towel around my body. When I open the door to the berth, I find it empty. A pair of jeans, T-shirt and underthings lie on the bed. On the floor, a pair of socks sticks out of deck shoes. It reminds me of the times Reece laid out my clothes. Everything around me reminds me of him.

I dress without thought and stare at the bed. When I close my eyes, I can still smell him surrounding me. Slipping on the deck shoes, I make my way back toward the cockpit.

THE MENTAL FOG LINGERS, GIVING ME NO SENSE OF TIME UNTIL I step into the cockpit. Over the bow, the first light of dawn peeks over the horizon. All around me, people move. Scrub brushes scrape across the deck. Water spills across the blood-stained wood. The last of the sick crew is being shuttled off the yacht. I stare at the almost placid sea.

Behind me, I sense the presence before the person speaks.

"Is there something I can help you with?" I ask without turning around.

"Yes, Ma'am. Mr. Kinkaid is on the sat phone. He's demanding to speak with you."

"Tell Mr. Kinkaid I will talk with him soon."

"It's the eighth time he's called, Ma'am."

I sigh deeply and turn.

"I'm sorry, I never asked your name." I look up at the man attired completely in black. It is unlike me not to know the surrounding personnel on my team. The thought brings with it the whirlwind memories of the last few days. At the house, our security melded into the background. It wasn't until we boarded the sailboat that I even noticed them, and even then Reece distracted me.

I look up at the man. Two thick sleeves of tattoos stick out from under his tight T-shirt. Dark sunglasses and a black operator's hat shield his gaze from me. His large frame towers over me by nearly five inches; he must be near six foot seven.

"John, Ma'am."

"Please, John, call me Atlas."

"I can't do that, Ms. Devereaux. Mr. Kinkaid would have my hide, and no offence, but he's scarier." A tight smile forms in a thin line across his lips.

"For now."

His brows knit in confusion as he hands me the sat phone.

"Atlas Devereaux." I speak with authority into the mouthpiece.

"Atlas, oh thank God! Are you okay?" Kade's voice rushes through the phone.

"I am physically fine, Thomas."

"Oh." He pauses as I use his first name. It is a sure sign nothing is right in my world.

"Things on the ground here are... chaotic and uncertain."

"I just got word Reece is being airlifted to Miami."

At the mention of his name, my breath catches.

Kade's tone turns from friendly to stoic as he reports the facts.

"According to my sources, the object missed his artery by a quarter of an inch. The application of pressure and a move to the recovery position saved his life."

My legs give out in that moment and strong hands help me to the deck.

"The jet will be on the tarmac for your arrival in four hours. Based on the information from my team, it will take you six hours to get back to port. Everything you need will be on the plane when you dock. Wheels will be up as soon as you are ready. We could get you back faster, but I think it is best to leave you on the yacht. A new crew will be aboard shortly to bring her home."

I nod at the phone, afraid if I speak, I won't be able to contain the emotions.

"Everyone on the new crew I know personally. They were in the general area at the time I put out the emergency call and are en route to you. We are still assessing how this happened."

"*The Art of War.*" The words slip past my lips as an explanation.

"Excuse me, Ma'am?"

"I was playing the wrong game. Actually, I didn't even realize it was a game. In some sick way, I seem to be the prize. The only tactics that will work are Sun Tzu. This is all a mind game, with deadly outcomes."

"I see." Kade's simple answer speaks volumes. "We'll get this bastard."

I bite hard into my lip to prepare for my next question and take a deep breath.

"Have you heard from Dominick?"

"We are still trying to locate him, Ma'am."

"He's not..." I can't complete the question.

"We don't know."

CHAPTER THIRTY-TWO

THE PHONE TUMBLES from my hand. Kade's faint voice calls from the lump of plastic and electronics. Large hands lift it from my lap.

"We've got her, Sir," John replies.

My lungs tighten, and I struggle to breathe. On wobbly legs, I move to stand. Each step carries me toward the bow of the boat.

"No, Sir."

"Yes, Sir."

I can hear the staccato replies behind me. Each step makes them fainter. I see the faint red outline of the blood pools and stumble. My knees slam into the deck and I crawl to the center, pull my knees to my chest, and stare out at the sea. Red skies herald the beginning of a treacherous day. Off to the port side, dark, angry clouds reflect my mood as gray lines streak from the sky.

The hard thud of boots across the deck draws my attention, but I do not turn to acknowledge them. When they approach my position, they pause and do not continue forward.

The quiet blankets the deck as people disappear, their chores and responsibilities complete. I hear the faint rumble of engines pull away from the boat. Below us, the sea swells angrily and tries to force the large yacht to roll on the white caps, but it stubbornly refuses to move on its moor.

Sometime later, I hear the approach of a tender. Voices echo through the boat. Soft footsteps move up the deck.

"Permission to come aboard, Ma'am," the new voice asks.

"Looks to me like you're already aboard," I reply drily without moving my eyes from the horizon.

"Yes, Ma'am. I am Captain Wilson. Mr. Kinkaid sent us."

I nod without a word.

"There's a squall coming up our port side. We need to get underway as soon as possible."

"Do what you must."

"Everyone on board needs to put on a PFD and clip in." The words have some faint meaning, and I nod but do not move from my position.

"I'll take care of it, Captain," John says from my other side.

"Very good."

I hear his footsteps retreat back toward the cockpit.

"Standby to weight anchor." The captain calls out the order.

Quick footsteps move up the deck and a young man appears in front of me. He reaches down into the locker and pulls up a handheld control. His hand moves in the air.

"Ready to weigh anchor." He follows up the signal.

The engines of the yacht rumble to life and vibrate the deck.

"Weigh anchor." The captain's voice carries on the edge of the wind.

"Weighing anchor!"

The loud sound of a large chain breaks through my unpleasant silence. Each link rattles and bounces as it draws into the locker. The crewman's hand never stops moving as the anchor is ripped from the sea. With a final bang, the anchor bounces to a stop.

"Ma'am, you need to put on your personal flotation device and don't even try to argue." His tone is friendly but stern. I can just imagine the discussion he had with Kade.

He hands me a slim U-shaped floatation device.

"If you go overboard, this device will automatically inflate. Should it fail to inflate, there is a red T-handle for inflation and a hose here should you need to fill it yourself. Make sure you place your legs through the leg straps and clip in to the jackline," he says and points to a long blue webbing running down either side of the deck.

I nod but do not move. My fingers trace across the stitching.

"Let me try this again, Ma'am. Either you get off your ass and move or I will strap you in myself."

I turn my head indignantly and a small smile pulls at the edge of my mouth as I imagine the threats and outrage Kade is putting everyone through right now.

He offers his hand to help me stand, and I accept it.

I step into the harness, pull it over my head, and buckle it across my chest. John pulls hard on the floatation device and nods in approval as he hands me the tether, which I've already attached to the jackline.

The first spatters of rain pepper the deck as I clip the line to the harness.

"Ready the mainsail!"

"Mainsail ready!"

"Raise the mainsail!"

The large sail climbs the mast, luffing angrily in the wind.

"Prepare to come about!" the captain calls over the winds.

"Ready!" a chorus of voices answer.

"Coming about!"

The large yacht turns through the wind and winches spin loudly as the sails move across the deck until the main fills and no longer slaps against the mast. In response, the boat heels to her side and we pick up speed with the force of the squall rising around us.

"Let's get you into a covered area, unless you enjoy being drenched," John says wryly.

I nod and make my way across the deck and down the side back toward the cockpit.

———

THE PASSAGE BACK TO PORT IS A BLUR AS THE SQUALL REFLECTS my mood and batters the boat. It dissipates just outside our mooring point and the crew scrambles to bring us to anchor. For most of the trip, I huddle in a corner of the cockpit. John's large frame is always hovering nearby.

A marina tender approaches the boat and bumps against the diving platform. My legs cramp as I stretch and trip over the edge of the gunwale. Strong hands catch me and prevent me from tipping forward into the sea.

"I've got you, Ma'am," John says as he sets me right on my feet, then hands me into the tender.

Once everyone is settled, the large inflatable turns toward the pier. Saltwater sprays across us as we rapidly skip across the water.

I give in to the darkness threatening to consume me and let it take my mind. Everything around me becomes a blur. John's short, quick orders compel my body to move, but they do not fully register.

At the end of the dock, he helps me into the back of a small van and steps forward to the driver's seat. He pulls away from the marina. The yacht soon fades in the distance as we drive to the airport.

The van moves back to the tarmac and stops at the bottom of the same private jet which started this insane adventure. I stare up at it. So many things have changed since I walked down those stairs and yet so much feels the same—I am still adrift. John opens my door and moves aside as I step out. He tosses the keys to a man walking up to the van and grabs two bags from the back.

At the bottom of the stairs, I hesitate and stare up at the yawning opening of the plane.

"In you go." John's low voice reverberates behind me.

I climb the stairs with laden legs.

Captain Reid stands just inside the cabin. I nod wordlessly as I pass and go toward the large seats. Behind me I hear John speak to him in a low voice, but I don't bother to listen. I sit and buckle the seatbelt across my lap as John stows the bags in the bin at the front, then takes a seat across from me.

The attendant runs through the safety procedures and I force a smile in her direction. When everyone is seated, the plane's engines spool up, and we surge forward as we move toward the runway.

I tighten my grip on the seat as the plane accelerates and lifts, smoothing into the air. My stomach drops and I let out a breath.

"Good afternoon, we are currently climbing to a cruising altitude of thirty-five thousand feet at an airspeed of six hundred miles per hour. The weather looks like we may be in for a few bumps for the first little bit, but it should be clear skies heading into Leesburg. Total flight three hours, forty-eight minutes. If you require anything, please don't hesitate to request it from your attendant."

When we reach our cruising altitude, a signal dings through the cabin and I hear the attendant unbuckle from her seat.

"May I offer a beverage?" she asks, and her voice is far too chipper for my mood.

I shake my head.

"She'll have a gin and tonic, doubled," John replies, and my head snaps toward him. "I'll have a glass of ice water, please."

He gives her a full-watt smile and I watch her melt as she turns back into the cabin.

"How dare you?" I hiss.

"How dare I what, Ma'am? Create a situation to take the edge off the trauma you've suffered? Give you a bit of liquid courage in the face of everything you are about to lift? How dare I step in and force you to march on when you are too weary to lift another foot?"

I glare at him.

"Kade told me you were head-strong, stubborn and after a crisis you close up."

"He knows me well."

"He's worried about you."

"I'll be fine," I fire back.

"That's a given, but will your world still be standing when you finally get to that point?"

I glare at him, but he just smiles back at me.

The attendant sets our drinks in front of us, looking from one to the other, then retreats quickly to the back of the cabin.

I am the first to look away. My gaze drifts toward the soft-looking clouds outside and the bright sunlight bathing the plane.

John stands up and I turn my attention to him. He grabs a duffel from the overhead compartment. It differs from either of the bags he carried onboard, and he sets it down beside me.

"Kade thought this might help."

I unzip the top of the bag and the spike of a five-inch heel peeks out.

"Smart man," I comment quietly.

John nods in agreement.

CHAPTER THIRTY-THREE

"KADE! What have you done to my club?" I roar, my five-inch heels clicking across the marble foyer.

"Alexandra?" The surprise in his voice tells me my return is unexpected. "We weren't expecting you back for a few more days."

Samantha's head jerks my way and an elbow pokes Kade in his ribs.

"How are..." My glare stops his question. In my domain I will not show any weakness. There is no running this time. This is my home and I will defend it. Before Reece I was lost, and now, even alone, I know my place in the world. It is my job to lift it and I will protect everything I have left in it.

I straighten my shoulders and look at the small group.

"I take my PR consultant, Atlas Devereaux with me to scout for another location out of country, of which you were well aware, and you let this place go to hell in a hand basket in a matter of a couple months." I shake my head in mock disapproval. Around me, the club is spotless. The membership is light, but it gives me hope that some things will return to normal.

I pray they will follow my lead.

The entire club watches the display.

Eyes bore into us from every direction as silence engulfs the room.

Kade and Samantha school their faces as I announce the reason for my disappearance, and I let out a grateful exhale.

"Well, if you were better at staying in touch, we might be able to run this place to your impossible standards," he challenges me.

"Watch your tone," I warn.

"My tone?" he says indignantly.

"Yes. Or did you forget my position in the short time I was gone?"

The air is thick with tension. This moment defines how hard the world will land on my shoulders. In front of me Kade plays his part with ease as he steps into my space. At the last second his eyes fall to the floor with a slight nod of his head.

"It's good to see you too, Ma'am." He takes the final steps forward and engulfs me in a bear hug before stepping back again.

A woman steps around Kade. His head bows slightly as she passes, and I don't miss the subtle gesture.

"I don't believe we've met. I'm Jessica." She holds her hand out.

I glance between her and Kade. He shrugs and I take her hand in a warm handshake.

"Jessica, this is Alexandra, the owner of this fine establishment. Alexandra, this is Officer Lawson. She's working the club's case," the big man says with an air of reverence.

I look back and forth between Officer Lawson and Kade.

"Shall we go to my office?" I offer. "Mr. Kinkaid, I presume the necessary reports are already on my desk."

A look of terror washes over Kade's face and I return it with a smirk, knowing there was no way he had all the information I needed.

"Yes, Ma'am, and more are being finished as we speak."

"Good. We've got quite a few things to discuss." I pivot and walk confidently toward my office without another word. Murmurs break out throughout the club. The sound of footsteps tells me everything I need to know.

Around me the murmurs turn to words. "Welcome back."

I nod politely and let my world settle back on my shoulders, wishing Reece was here to help me shoulder the load. *Hopefully soon*, I reassure myself.

PLEA FROM THE AUTHOR

I am so glad you've reached the end of the book and hope you enjoyed it. Thank you for giving me your valuable entertainment time. It is readers like you who make writing such an amazing experience.

If you enjoyed the book, I hope you will leave a review.

Be the First to Know

Want news, pre-order announcements or stuff?

www.SacchariaMayer.com

Want to catch up on all my behind the scenes, current WIPs, side projects and early announcements? Become a Patreon of the Arts.

Sappharia Mayer's Patreons of the Arts

Feel free to reach out to me on any of my social media.

BB bookbub.com/authors/sappharia-mayer

twitter.com/sapphariamayer

pinterest.com/sapphariamayer

amazon.com/author/sapphariamayer

instagram.com/sapphariamayer

SUBMIT TO ME- CHAPTER 1
EMPYREAN CLUB- THE ATLAS COLLECTION BOOK 4

THE INSISTENT BLARE of the phone as it walked across the nightstand in a constant vibration pulled Kade out of the edge of sleep. It screamed its emergency and demanded his attention. He glanced at the clock and noted he'd only laid down less than two hours ago. Fighting instinct, he let the phone continue until it died. He breathed a sigh of relief and punched the pillow. Just as he settled, the phone vibrated again, and he cursed under his breath, rolled over and grabbed the phone.

Empyrean Command Center the bright screen announced the caller. He slid a large thumb across the screen and grit his teeth.

"Kade!" His voice was harsh and hoarse.

He'd run another long shift. As the head of security for the club, it was his job to keep everyone safe. His most recent failure to protect the owner, *Alexandra*, added to his already heavy burden and guilt.

"Sir, we have a situation." The edge in the voice on the other end of the phone was clear but told him a little about the problem.

"Spit it out. I'm in no mood to guess our most recent incident and decide it if is an actual problem or if you all are too incompetent to know the difference."

"Sir, I need you to come to the club ASAP. I'd rather not discuss it on an open line."

Kade ran his hand through his barely there high and tight. A scowl marred his face.

"I'm twenty mikes out," he acknowledged.

"Roger that."

The line when dead and Kade rolled to sit up on the edge of the bed. Good thing he'd showered last night. It looked like it would be another long day. He walked over to his closet, grabbed a pair of black BDUs and a club security polo. He took less than five minutes to dress and grab his keys as he headed for the door and headed to the garage.

The bright red Tesla roadster called to him. He could imagine pushing his irritation through her on the way to the club as he ripped through the gears and took the corners hard.

Instead, he opted for the large black Cadillac Escalade. In one smooth motion, he hit start on the remote and the garage door responded. He slid behind the wheel and pulled out of the driveway. As soon as he was on the road, he hit the accelerator and pushed the large vehicle towards the club he'd left recently.

Ten minutes later, he pulled up the back gate, which opened immediately in response to his RFID car tag. The long narrow road wasn't as elegant as the primary entrance, but the service road provided the perfect vantage point as he approached the club.

From this angle, everything was quiet. The light fog of the morning sat just off the ground, giving the scene and an ethereal look. He pulled the SUV up to the parking garage gate and waited for it to respond. Beside him, the security camera panned down and seconds later the garage door began its decent.

He pulled through the parking structure and backed into the open space marked, "Reserved for Security Director."

As soon as the engine died, his door opened. A young man passed a cup of coffee to him and a radio.

"Sit rep," he commanded.

"Sir, a threat was posted on the front door."

"What kind of threat?" Kade asked, as he accepted the coffee and climbed out of the driver's seat. He didn't stop moving towards the club door as he heard the SUV's door shut and reverberate around the structure. The thump of boots echoed in his wake as the young man worked to keep up.

Kade stopped and turned. He glared at the man before him.

"I said, what kind of threat, boot?" He growled, his irritation sitting right at the surface.

"Someone stabbed a bloody knife into the front door with a threatening note."

Kade turned toward the door, swiped his badge, and headed to the command center.

"Who's on fire watch?"

"Tanner. He's in the command center reviewing the tapes. He's called in all personnel."

"Roger."

He continued through the club as he connects his radio and settles his ear piece and clicked to set the current channel. His mind struggled

Kade clicked the button and spoke into his mic.

"Radio check," he called and released the button.

"Five by five." A voice answered in response.

Satisfied his radio was in good working order, he took a long swig of his black coffee, thankful for the dark elixir's power to put him back on his feet. He desperately needed sleep. Between his constant nightmares and the developing security situation surrounding the club, he never seemed to catch enough time before something else needed his immediate attention.

His heavy boots echoed off the marble foyer tile as he made his way through the club.

"Does anyone have eyes on Kade?" The radio crackled in his ear and he groaned inwardly.

"Go for Kade."

"What's your twenty?"

"Head to Command, over."

"Kade, this is Command. Code Yellow at the front gate."

"Copy that. Redirecting."

He turned toward Dean. He was new to the team and everyone referred to him as boot.

"With me," he commanded and pivoted to the side door. He didn't want to disturb the site of investigation.

"On your six, Sir."

The two men walked out through the side service entrance of the sizable house. The brisk morning air helped him clear the last remnants of sleep from his mind. Years of military training forced an automatic calm as the adrenaline coursed through him. As they approached the circular driveway he looked out towards the gate. White specks of vehicles pulled near the entrance.

Kade grabbed the small tablet housed in his side pocket. A couple taps later, the screen lit up with the image from the front gate. Three news vans were setting up. Satellite dishes reached towards the sky.

"Whisky Tango Foxtrot," he swore under this breath and turned toward the front door.

Someone had buried a large ka-bar knife deep in the center of the right double door. Thick plops of blood dripped from the handle marring the marble entrance. Under the knife's tip, a piece of paper fluttered in the breeze.

"Kade to Command."

"Go for Command."

"Sir, we've got incoming black and whites."

Frustration tightened every muscle in his body. The situation was spinning out of control faster than he could get a handle on it.

"Command, did you call them?"

"Negative."

"This is becoming a cluster fuck," he grumbles and then clicks the button on his radio. "Command, get Gabriel on the horn. This situation is FUBAR."

"Copy that."

Kade lifted the tablet. With a swipe, he aimed it at the front door and worked to take pictures from every angle to study later. If it was from Edmund, then at least it meant Alexandra was safe. On the other hand, the news outlets in front of the club also meant there was an incoming public relations nightmare.

"Black and whites are demanding entrance." The radio crackled.

"Give me three mikes and let them through," he called back.

"Roger."

He turned toward Dean.

"Stay frosty. It's about to get intense."

The young man nodded. He'd hired dean as a favor to a friend. When he tried to join the military, he'd was rejected based on an undiagnosed knee deformity. The kid needed structure and discipline in his life, and Kade took him under his wing. He'd learned quickly, and Kade had high hopes he'd be a valuable asset to the team.

"Incoming." The voice crackled over the radio.

"Roger," Kade replied. "All stations, this is Kade. Impose radio silence. Over."

The radio echoed with several calls of "Copy that" and "Roger". Then fell silent as the police cars pulled into the circular drive.

Kades pulls his phone out of his pocket as he watches two unmarked cars roll down the driveway towards him while two marked cars stayed at the gate. With two quick taps, he pulled up Samantha's phone number and waited for it to connect.

"There better be an excellent reason for this call," her sleepy voice sang through the line.

"You better turn on the tv. I think we will need your expertise-fast," Kade replied.

"What's going on?" The sudden alertness in her tone gave him a moment of control in his spiraling world.

"Just turn on the television. You're the public relations person. I think we're getting ready to have a genuine problem."

"You've got to give me more details than that, man," she demanded.

"Later. Just do your job," he interrupted and ended the call as the cars rolled to a stop in front of him.

The captain of the police force stepped out of the first car and walked up the stairs.

"Looks like ya'll have a bit of a situation, Kade," the older man smiled and held out his hand. Because of the clientele and the nature of the business, he'd worked closely with the local police department for the last several years.

"Indeed," Kade answered noncommittally.

The sound of a car door shutting brought both men's attention to a woman stepping out of the other car. She was small, almost fragile, in the looming shadow of the enormous house. Her suit hugged every curve of her well toned body. His eyes lingered down to her bare legs and back up again. There was something about her that pulled on Kade's need to protect and set him on edge.

"This is detective Lawson. She'll be running our investigation," the captain said as the woman made her way up the front marble stairs.

When she reached the top, she stuck out her hand.

"And you are?" She asked.

Kades enormous hand engulfed hers and their touch sent a buzz straight to his groin, making him scowl.

"Kade. Director of Security."

Her eyebrow quirked and her eyes narrowed at his short direct answer

"Well, Kade," she tried out his name and scrunched her nose like it wasn't quite right. "We got an anonymous call, there was a possible murder on the property."

"A murder? Really?"

"Yes. Do you mind if I have a look around?" Her tone was even, giving away nothing.

"Actually, I mind."

"You know, this can go down easy for both of us or I can make it a shit show," she challenged.

"I see," Kade replied evenly. For a long time they stared each other down. Her assumption of control was hot as hell. He continued to look down at the diminutive woman. The air practically sizzled with tension when both refused to backdown.

He broke eye contact and reached for the button on his ear piece. Out of the corner of his eye, he saw her take a mental victory lap as her shoulders straightened. The move pushed her pert breast forward under her jacket and he internally moaned.

'Get it together,' he scolded himself and pushed the button.

"All teams secure comms on Channel 7. Secure posts 3,7,9,12 and 15. Secure comms only," he said into the radio.

He watched her face fall as he looked up.

"Now. How can I help you today, Detective?" He said in a neutral tone that belied the mass of things running through his body.

4

Kade waited a long heartbeat before she spoke again.

"Shall we start over?" She asked, forcing a smile across her face.

He loved the fire in her eyes. There was something about her that made him want to challenge her and watch her rise to meet it.

"Sure."

"Mr. Kade, I'm Detective Jessica Lawson. Someone called in an anonymous tip and told us there was a bloody knife and a potential murder on these grounds. I'd like your permission to investigate these allegations so we can both get on with our day." She let a slight smile play across her mouth.

At six foot two, he was almost a foot taller than her, but the confidence and authority told him she wasn't intimidate by the difference in size.

"You look young to be a detective," he said, the words rolling off his tongue without thought.

"Yep. A small, delicate, fragile flower just needing a powerful man to protect me," she said in a sickly sweet tone.

Embarrassment registered across Kade's face.

"I didn't mean too...," he started.

"Yes, you did. Just like every male before you." She shook her head. "Now, if you are quite done with your self-important evaluation of my skills based solely on my size, can we get on with this investigation? I've got more important things to do than to have a 'my dick is bigger than yours' contest. Besides, I can strap mine on in the necessary size and shape. Unfortunately, for you, yours is original equipment and can't be altered to suit, so I hope it's a good size."

With that, she let her eyes dip down to his crotch for a long lingering look. He felt his cock grow hard under her scrutiny and breathed a sigh of relief when she looked up again.

"And yes, in fact, mine are brass. Is yours?" She smirked.

Beside him, the captain laughed at the exchange.

"Do you let all your detectives talk to people like this?" Kade looked over at him.

"Don't think you can handle it, big guy?" The captain slapped him on the back and chuckled.

Kade rolled his eyes and looked back down at the detective.

"What do you want to do from here?"

The loaded question made his mind go to all the things he'd like to do with her behind this door. He shook his head at his wayward thoughts, shoving them out of his way in an attempt reigned by the sudden fire in his libido.

"Let me get my forensics team in here and collect evidence. Then search the grounds to see if there's been an actual crime or if this is all an elaborate hoax to bring media attention."

Kade ran a frustrated hand through his hair.

"If we find nothing, I'll make a press statement and scatter the roaches," she said with a shrug. "Or, I can walk out there tell them the situation is under investigation and we're going for a search warrant. I'm sure your clientele will love the constant media attention and the fear of being recognized as they come through those gates. Or maybe they won't and business will dry up." She pointed toward the gate and the building media presence he knew was already there. "Balls in your court, Mr. Kade."

"Just Kade."

"Say again." She looked up at him.

The sparkle in her pale grey, almost silver eyes, took him aback. He shook his head to regain his composure.

"My name is Kade, just Kade," he growled, his own frustration clear.

"Ok, just Kade. Shall we get this show on the road?"

"Bring in your forensics team, Ma'am. Then you can go tell them media it was all a hoax."

"Fantastic. I knew we'd work well together," she said with a triumphant smile, but her tone remained even and deadpan. Jessica picked up her radio and issued the order.

Kade punched a new secure channel into his own radio as he watched her.

"Let the forensics vehicle through, Command."

"Copy that," replied a disembodied voice.

"I'll let you get on with it then. Dean, here, will get you anything you need." He nodded towards the young man who'd followed him out earlier.

"Captain. Detective Lawson," he said as he nodded to them both and walked down the stairs.

After that encounter, he needed a cold shower, but first, he needed to find out exactly what was going on around here.

SUBMIT TO ME (THE ATLAS COLLECTION BOOK 4)

"Semper Fi" wasn't just a saying for Thomas Kinkaid. As the head of security at the DC region's most exclusive and luxurious kink club, he put his responsibilities first. When Alexandra disappeared after being stalked and threatened by a client, he'd failed in his duty. Now it was time to get this FUBAR situation under control. The weight of his guilt was already heavy enough without adding these new developments.

At five foot four, Jessica Lawson knew what it was like to fight for her place in the world. She works twice as hard to get to the next level and demanded the respect she deserves. As a detective, she's focused on the only thing she could control- her career. When she got the call about a threatening post and a possible murder at a local high end BDSM club, she was the first one to volunteer. Everything about this case spoke to her and desires she didn't reveal to anyone.

When the two meet, sparks fly but she wants a man who will submit to her. Arrogance and self-assuredness pours off Kade and there's no way this former marine was going to sink to his knees for anyone. But there's something about Kade that make her body sing and her mind wants to investigate the reason for the haunted look in his eyes. Just maybe, they'll find the right steps for both of them.

Pre-order now! Submit to Me

ALSO BY SAPPHARIA MAYER

EMPYREAN CLUB SERIES

The Atlas Collection

Mask Me (Book 1)

Master Me (Book 2)

Reveal me (Book 3)

Submit to Me (Book 4)

Play with Me (Book 5)

Mind Games Series - Coming soon!

His Toy Collection

Becoming His Toy

His Toy for the Weekend

His Toy is Going Deeper

His Toy is Trusting Him

ABOUT THE AUTHOR

Sappharia Mayer's erotic romance comes from years of experience in dynamic and various play in the BDSM/Kink lifestyle. She portrays the dance of power exchange relationships with a passion that pushes her characters, and readers, outside their comfort zone, making them squirm, cry, laugh and learn to see things in a whole new way.

Living around the metro area of the nation's capital gives her an up close view of politics and power on a global scale. She loves to delve deep into her worlds and indulge in her various passions, which may or may not include instigating fun *trouble* with her warped sense of humor. If you love romance based in power exchanges with hot kinky sex, then check out Sappharia's books.